# Dear Hank Williams

## KIMBERLY WILLIS HOLT

SQUARE
FISH
Christy Ottaviano Books
Henry Holt and Company
New York

*This story is dedicated to my grandfather
Henry Mitchell,
June 2, 1915–July 7, 2014.*

SQUARE
FISH

An Imprint of Macmillan
175 Fifth Avenue
New York, NY 10010
mackids.com

Square Fish and the Square Fish logo are trademarks of Macmillan and
are used by Henry Holt and Company, LLC under license from Macmillan.

Our books may be purchased in bulk for promotional, educational, or business use.
Please contact your local bookseller or the Macmillan Corporate and Premium
Sales Department at (800) 221-7945 ext. 5442 or by e-mail at
MacmillanSpecialMarkets@macmillan.com.

Library of Congress Cataloging-in-Publication Data
Holt, Kimberly Willis.
Dear Hank Williams / Kimberly Willis Holt.
pages     cm
"Christy Ottaviano Books."
Summary: Assigned to write to a pen pal, eleven-year-old Tate, who lives in
Rippling Creek, Louisiana, in 1948, writes to her favorite country singer,
sharing her dream of becoming a singer and revealing that her mother is in prison.
ISBN 978-1-250-07978-7 (paperback)     ISBN 978-1-62779-443-5 (ebook)
[1. Family life—Louisiana—Fiction.   2. Singing—Fiction.   3. Williams, Hank,
1923–1953—Fiction.   4. Louisiana—History—20th century—Fiction.
5. Letters—Fiction.]   I. Title.
PZ7.H74023De 2015     [Fic]—dc23     2014036808

Originally published in the United States by Christy Ottaviano
Books/Henry Holt and Company, LLC
First Square Fish Edition: 2016
Book designed by Patrick Collins
Square Fish logo designed by Filomena Tuosto

1   3   5   7   9   10   8   6   4   2

AR: 5.0 / LEXILE: 820L

Dear Hank Williams,

WELCOME TO THE great state of Louisiana! My name is Tate P. Ellerbee, and I'm writing you from Rippling Creek in Rapides Parish. That's a long way from Shreveport, but our radio is tuned to KWKH every Saturday night. I've been listening to you on the *Louisiana Hayride* ever since you first performed on the show last month. When you sang "Move It On Over," swear to sweet Sally, I felt a wiggle travel down my whole body. The upbeat chorus made my little brother, Frog, and me dance around the room. Uncle Jolly said he'd heard better singers, but don't pay him no mind. He's a lovesick man.

Aunt Patty Cake liked your song too. She stared up from her copy of *True Confessions* and asked, "What do you reckon he looks like?"

Today was the first day of school. My new teacher, Mrs. Kipler, has glasses as thick as Coca-Cola bottles.

I guess she's real smart and wore out her eyes from all that reading. I had to bite my tongue to resist the urge to suggest Delightfully Devine's black eyeliner. It would be just the thing to bring out her brown eyes.

Now, here's the exciting part of this letter. Mrs. Kipler told the class, "This year new worlds will unfold in front of you, and you'll see your own world through fresh eyes." Right that minute I was ready to pack a suitcase for the trip. Then she said it would happen through writing letters to a pen pal.

Some of my classmates groaned. Wallace Scott groaned the loudest, but he's a bully and I guess he wanted to start the year off reminding us of that fact.

Mrs. Kipler told us we could pick our own pen pal but that she hoped we'd let her assign each of us one. She promised they would be from a special place.

That minute I knew exactly who my pen pal was going to be. Guess who, Hank Williams? I've picked you! Since you sing on the *Louisiana Hayride* and I'm going to sing at the Rippling Creek May Festival Talent Contest, we already have something in common. You and I are going to be great buddies. It's funny how things work out, because before Mrs. Kipler told us about our pen pal project, I'd planned to write you a letter. The Monday after I heard you sing, I rode my bicycle over to the post office and asked the postmaster, Mr. Snyder, to look up the address for the Shreveport Municipal Auditorium. He finally gave it to me, but not before I answered a bunch of nosy questions about why I wanted it. (If you ask me, Mr. Snyder knows entirely too much about everyone around Rippling Creek.)

This letter will have to be top secret because Mrs. Kipler asked us not to write yet. She's assigning topics for our first few letters so that we can learn to write interesting correspondence. She clearly doesn't know a thing about me, because I *am* an interesting person. And interesting people always have something curious to write about.

I'll write again, real soon (probably tomorrow).

Your fan and new pen pal,
Tate P. Ellerbee

Dear Hank Williams,

TODAY MRS. KIPLER ASKED if any of us had chosen a pen pal. You'll never believe this: I was the only kid who'd picked one. A lot of people in this world don't have gumption, but I do. Here's the funny thing, though. When I told her your name, Mrs. Kipler scrunched up her face and asked, "Is he a distant cousin?" I had to explain that you sang every Saturday night on the *Louisiana Hayride*. She looked as dumb as a bell without a ring.

"Don't you have a radio?" I asked her. She didn't answer. She kept asking me questions, wanting to know how I knew you. "I'm going to get to know him," I told her, "because we're going to be pen pals."

Her voice got all soft. "Tate, let's talk about this at recess."

Then Mrs. Kipler faced the class and told them she had a very important announcement about who their pen pals could be. Somehow she'd made connections with a teacher all the way over in Japan who had students who wanted to write to American children.

Wallace Scott stood. "Japan?"

"Correct," Mrs. Kipler said. "Now sit down, Wallace."

He was not happy about that choice. Wallace's daddy's uncle died in Pearl Harbor, so I guess you can't blame him for thinking that way.

Mrs. Kipler's brains must have frizzled from her last perm. We just got out of a war with those folks. I'm not about to share my life with the enemy. I remember when I was four years old, the soldiers from Camp Claiborne marched past our house in the mornings. Aunt Patty Cake would have a pot of coffee ready for them. Before we saw them, we heard the *stomp, stomp* sounds of their boots pounding the road. When we did, we'd walk outside, Aunt Patty Cake with the coffee, Momma with the cups and cream, and me with the spoons.

The men's leader would yell, "At ease!" and the men would settle on the side of the road. Aunt Patty Cake made her way down the line pouring coffee. They'd have to take turns with the cups because we only had five, but they didn't seem to mind. Nobody had ever asked us to do it. Aunt Patty Cake said it was a small way of doing our part.

Once, one of the soldiers lifted me and settled me on his shoulders. He marched up and down the stretch of road in front of our house. *Stomp, stomp, stomp.* I remember noticing tears in his eyes when he put me down. Later I asked Aunt Patty Cake and Momma, "Why was that man crying?" Aunt Patty Cake said, "He probably has a little girl like you at home, Tate."

So you see, Mr. Williams, even if you weren't my pen pal, I couldn't write someone from Japan. I'd feel like I was betraying those men who passed by our house every morning.

Which brings me to the next point. Mrs. Kipler said in our first letter we should tell you about ourselves and where we live. She said, "You may not think you live in a fascinating place, but to other people, especially those living across the world, Rippling Creek is exotic."

Exotic? I'm an optimist. I look at a glass half-full, but Mrs. Kipler must see it all fogged up. Rippling Creek is anything but exotic. And despite that Mrs. Kipler tried to convince me at recess that writing you was a waste of time when I could be learning about another culture, I'm going to keep you as my pen pal. So don't worry, Hank Williams. You and I will be closer than double-first cousins because we'll learn about each other and how much we have in common. So without any delay, I'll tell you a little about me and the anything-but-exotic Rippling Creek.

First of all, I've got plain brown hair and brown eyes, which seems ordinary, but people say I'm starting to look like my momma. My prayers must be working. I know I'm supposed to pray for the sick and the lost souls, but I can't help it. Every night I squeeze my eyes shut and whisper to heaven, "Please let me be beautiful and sing pretty like Momma." Since I'm only eleven, there's hope for me yet. By the way, what do you look like, Hank Williams?

Rippling Creek is a speck on the Louisiana state map about eighteen miles south of Alexandria. Don't picture a busy place like New York City or New Orleans. Most of us live in the country. Hardly anyone lives in town. The town of Rippling Creek has a post office and one gas station. You can't include Hazel's Cut and Curl, because her shop is inside her house on Fish Hatchery Road.

Rippling Creek has tall longleaf pine trees everywhere that give off a clean scent like fresh-cut grass. Even though it's named Rippling Creek, we don't have a creek here named that. There is Hurricane Creek, Catfish Creek, Marty Porter Creek, Boot Creek, and No-Name Creek. If I was mayor, I'd call No-Name Creek Rippling Creek, but I'm not mayor. When I am, that's the first thing I'll do.

For now, I live on Canton Cemetery Road, straight across from the cemetery. Our home is the little red brick house with the torn screen porch door (that Uncle Jolly never gets around to fixing).

Living a stone's throw from the cemetery may seem depressing to you, but the location is actually prime real estate. It's the only place you'll eventually see almost everyone from these here parts. Every few weeks someone is bound to die, and practically everybody around Rippling Creek attends their funeral. Not me. I don't go to funerals. It's not because I'm afraid I'll cry, either. I'm not the crying type. I like to think of the deceased before they became that way. I reckon they'd like me to remember them that way too.

That doesn't stop other people in this house from going, though. Aunt Patty Cake is the queen of funeral-goers. Every time someone dies, she'll not only go to their funeral, she'll show up at their family's house later with a pecan pie. And when Uncle Jolly isn't working as a supervisor at Hopkins' Azalea Nursery (where they grow the prettiest azaleas in central Louisiana), he's the week-end cemetery groundskeeper. Saturdays, he mows the lawn and tidies up the grave sites. He tries to enlist me as his helper. "No sirree," I tell him. I don't want to spend my Saturdays throwing away dead flowers.

Uncle Jolly's not the only person asking me to go to the cemetery on a regular basis. Mrs. Applebud, who lives next door, wants me to accompany her on her two o'clock visits. I feel awful bad about her husband dying, but whenever she asks, I always tell her, "No, ma'am. Thank you, kindly." I can see all I want of the cemetery from my front yard. That doesn't stop her from asking, though. Whenever I notice it's almost two o'clock, I hide. Thank goodness she's predictable like everything else in Rippling Creek.

Here's what I mean. Every morning, at seven o'clock, Mr. Gayle Rockfire drops by for a quick cup of coffee with Uncle Jolly and Aunt Patty Cake. And each school day, Frog and I catch the bus out front at eight o'clock. The Missouri Pacific passes through our town at nine thirty, one o'clock, and five o'clock and in the middle of the night at three thirty a.m. And in case you forget, the engineer sounds that awful whistle at the crossings. Rudy Branson throws the *Alexandria Town Talk* at the end of our driveway at four o'clock every afternoon except Sunday. And come Sunday, every person I've ever known in my entire life (except Uncle Jolly) is sitting on a pew in Rippling Creek Southern Baptist Church. So as you can see, life in Rippling Creek is predictable, predictable, predictable.

Frog is the biggest eight-year-old pest in Rapides Parish, but if it weren't for my little brother, I'd die of boredom. And since Aunt Patty Cake won't let me have a dog, he'll have to do.

Trying not to suffer from
my predictable surroundings,
Tate P. Ellerbee

September 3, 1948

Dear Hank Williams,

MRS. KIPLER'S BIG PLAN about getting Japanese pen pals for everyone didn't seem to go like she'd hoped. Almost every kid came to class today with a different pen pal in mind. Everyone except Coolie Roberts and Theo Grace Thibodeaux, but they always forget their homework anyway. Mrs. Kipler looked like someone who didn't get any cards in her Valentine box. I have to admit, when the kids shared their pen pals' names, I could see why she was disappointed.

Verbia Calhoon picked her grandmother who lives in an old plantation home in Baton Rouge. Big deal! Most of the other kids selected their uncles, aunts, or cousins who live around Louisiana. The only person who picked someone out of state was Wallace Scott, who chose a cousin from Bay St. Louis, Mississippi.

You could have heard a fly land on the windowsill

when Wallace puffed out his chest and said, "My daddy said you're a Red communist if you choose to write anyone from Japan." He narrowed his eyes and stared around the class like he was daring someone to object.

The room grew quiet except for the sound of a few nervous kids' desks scraping against the floor.

Mrs. Kipler stared at Wallace. She said, "The war is over."

Wallace stared back. Nobody can do the staredown like Wallace. He didn't blink once.

Finally Mrs. Kipler turned away and told us to get out our arithmetic books. None of my classmates selected anybody near as exciting as you, Hank Williams, someone who I believe will be very famous one day. I have a radar for good talent. You can bank on it.

> Banking on the future of
> the sure-to-be-famous
> Hank Williams,
> Tate P. Ellerbee

PS—Please write back soon.

September 8, 1948

Dear Hank Williams,

I ASKED MRS. KIPLER if we had to share our letters with her, and she said, "No, though I hope you will. I think we will all grow from learning about other people, but I realize letters are personal possessions." That's what she said. Here's what I think: Mrs. Kipler is like most people around Rippling Creek—nosy about other folks' business. But she knows that reading other people's mail is against the law. Plain and simple. Mrs. Kipler doesn't want to get arrested.

Don't worry, Hank Williams, I won't share our letters. Who knows what could happen after we've been writing for a while? I might tell you some big secret, or you might tell me something that happens behind the scenes during the *Louisiana Hayride*. So feel free to write any and all gossip.

The only person who has had a response from her

pen pal is Verbia Calhoon. Wouldn't you know it? As expected, she came to school and bragged, bragged, bragged. She asked Mrs. Kipler if she could read hers aloud. Mrs. Kipler looked as pleased as punch and said, "Why, certainly, Verbia."

Verbia made such a production of standing, smoothing her skirt, tossing her blond curls, and reading her letter filled with boring details. How interesting could an old lady be? Her grandmother wrote about how she got her hair done and went to lunch with her old-lady friends at the Capitol's cafeteria. Mrs. Kipler got a big kick out of that part. She stopped Verbia's reading and reminded us that it was our state Capitol in Baton Rouge where Verbia's grandmother had eaten. When I got home, I told Frog about her letter. He fell fast asleep. The only interesting part was when her grandmother said she was going to buy her a French poodle. I hate to admit it, but that part made me jealous. It's not fair that somebody like Verbia can get a dog and I don't have a chance in the world of owning one. I'd be the perfect dog owner.

Mrs. Kipler said this week we're supposed to write to our pen pals about our family. My family would take a dozen letters to explain, but I'll do my best to squeeze it into one. Here we go!

My momma is in the picture-show business. That's why she's been away so long. She's busy starring in a film. When she comes home, she will buy me all kinds of pretty dresses and shoes. The kind that Verbia Calhoon wears. I'd tell you Momma's name, but Aunt Patty Cake doesn't like me to talk about her to anyone. I guess she thinks it's bragging. And I wouldn't want to ever be accused of boasting like those Calhoons.

I can tell you this. Momma always smells like gardenias, and she's beautiful. She has the sort of hair that women ask for at Hazel's Cut and Curl but walk out of the beauty shop looking like young chickens starting to shed their soft feathers. They look kind of blotchy. That's because they made the mistake of agreeing to a Toni perm from Hazel. Some folks say Momma's a dead ringer for Vivien Leigh. And she can sing so pretty. That's where I get my talent. She always seems to have another life going on inside her head. Sometimes I'll catch her in a daze, wearing a mysterious smile. Whenever I ask, "Momma, what are you thinking about?" she'll usually say, "Oh, I guess I was a million miles over yonder." Now it feels that way because she's been gone so long.

My daddy is a photographer, and he travels the world, taking pictures of lions in Africa and blue-ribbon jars of bread-and-butter pickles at state fairs. You've probably seen his photographs in *Life* magazine or *National Geographic*. He forgot to pack his pair of lace-up boots, and Frog insists on wearing them everywhere, but they are too big for him. I'd reveal who my daddy is, but again, I can't because of Aunt Patty Cake. She's the boss. With both of our parents away most of the year, Frog and me live with her and Uncle Jolly.

Are you wondering why we're living with my great-aunt and -uncle instead of our grandparents? Well, it's because of the most tragic story. You see, Momma is not the only famous singer in our family. My grandparents were well known in the church world. They were Dewright and Dottie, the Gospel Sweethearts. On their way home from singing at a revival in Waxahaxie, Texas, their car got a flat. As if that wasn't bad enough, they had the sour luck of it happening right around the bend in the road. A grocery truck didn't see their car and swerved toward them. Grandpa and Grandma were killed instantly.

Once, I asked Uncle Jolly about that evening. His eyes got all watery, and he said, "I still can't step foot in a church for fear that I'll hear the choir singing 'Just a Little Talk with Jesus.'" That was my grandparents' theme song. The offering plate overflowed whenever they sang it. Sad subjects tend to stay buried in this house, so I never ask about them anymore.

After they died, Aunt Patty Cake raised Momma. She was already raising her little brother, my uncle Jolly. He's a lot younger than Aunt Patty Cake and more like a big brother to Momma than an uncle.

Momma says Aunt Patty Cake was a looker in her day, but I can't see any trace of it. She's tall like Momma and is on the skinny side. Her salt-and-pepper hair is twisted on top of her head and held in place with about a hundred bobby pins. She doesn't wear much makeup herself, only a quick swipe of Rose Petal Pink lipstick (if she remembers). Which is mighty peculiar when you consider she's a sales representative for Delightfully Devine Beauty Products.

Aunt Patty Cake is like the sun. No matter what happens, you know that when you wake up, the sun is going to be there. Oh, there may be clouds trying to block it from shining, but the sun will be up in the sky, a big ball of fire burning, no matter what. The sun is so stubborn, the moon has a time getting rid of it. And when the sun finally slips past the horizon, you know it's there waiting to rise again. That's Aunt Patty Cake. Some folks call her dependable and find that an admirable quality, but I think it's better to possess some mystery, like Momma and me.

Aunt Patty Cake is strict about house rules. She's never written them down, but I know the list by heart. Here are the top three:

1. Do your chores without being asked.
2. Be nice to your little brother. (No matter what he does!)
3. No pets, especially dogs. (Even if it's the sweetest, best dog on the planet Earth that would never, ever dig up her flower garden or poop on the porch or stink from dog sweat.)

As you might've guessed from his name, Uncle Jolly has a big belly that hides his belt buckle. He has chubby cheeks that people probably wanted to pinch when he was a baby, but now they're starting to droop south. If there is anything Uncle Jolly is talented at, it's getting his heart broken. His first girlfriend left him for another feller a long time ago. Ever since then, Uncle Jolly seems to be addicted to heartbreak. He falls in love faster than Aunt Patty Cake burns toast. (Every time she makes it!) Almost as quick as Uncle Jolly falls in love, the woman breaks his heart.

That's when Uncle Jolly drives to the Wigwam and partakes in his second love—whiskey. We know Uncle Jolly has had his heart broken when we discover sofa cushions scattered on the floor and Aunt Patty Cake's straight chair pointing legs up. He leaves a trail through the mess where he's staggered to his bedroom. Aunt Patty Cake calls it "Jolly's Path of Heartbreak Destruction."

These days, Uncle Jolly has a girlfriend— Dolores Stanfield. She calls her hair "auburn," but it's as purple as an eggplant. And she may be skinny up top, but her behind is wide enough for a picture show to play on it. She's as prissy as they come. When I first met her, she held out her hand daintily as if she wanted me to kiss it. I squeezed and shook hard. Her fingers were icicles. She laughed like she'd swallowed a hairpin and said, "Cold hands. Warm heart." I can tell you for a fact, that ain't the case. So, Mr. Williams, don't pay any mind to Uncle Jolly's opinion of your singing. He can't pick a good woman or a great singer. The only thing Uncle Jolly is an expert at is plant cuttings.

Last but not least, let me introduce you to my little brother, Frog. No, that's not his real name. His birth name is James Irwin after Uncle Jolly, but before Frog learned to walk, he learned to jump. He would squat, keeping his palms pressed on the floor. Then he'd lift his behind, bounce a few times, and leap forward. He'd work so hard at it, his cheeks puffing up like a frog's. So he came by the name real honest. I have a few other names for him—Devil, Pest, Rascal, Brat, Troublemaker, Villain, Holy Terror, Scamp, Monkey Brain. Usually I call him Frog.

He thinks most food smells funny. Sometimes before going to the dinner table, he sneaks into the bathroom and dabs Uncle Jolly's Vicks VapoRub under his nostrils. He claims it keeps him from smelling food he doesn't like and getting sick to his stomach.

Frog acts like he's my shadow and follows me everywhere, wearing our daddy's big ole work boots, all the time asking, "Whatcha doing, Tate?" or "Whatcha thinking, Tate?" I wish he had a friend his age that lived next door instead of Mrs. Applebud, who's younger than the moon but older than anyone buried in Canton Cemetery (except for Mr. Applebud). If Frog had a pal, maybe he wouldn't be asking "Whatcha, whatcha" all the time.

Hank Williams, did you have a pesky little brother? If so, please tell me that they outgrow this stage.

Well, that's my family. We may not be perfect, but as Uncle Jolly says, we're like flypaper. We couldn't get unstuck from each other if we wanted. We're together through the good and bad. Swear to sweet Sally, we are.

Until next time,
Tate P. Ellerbee

PS—Please write back soon. Half the class have received letters back from their pen pals.

Dear Hank Williams,

DON'T YOU BELIEVE there are some downright evil people in this world? For example, a certain person I know with the initials V.C. is a perfect example of how some people may look pretty on the outside, but they are uglier than a mud fence on the inside.

This afternoon at school, ~~Verbia~~ V.C. announced that she was having a back-to-school sleepover party at her house. She handed out pink invitations. Every girl received one before lunch. Every girl except me. I was just thinking who'd want to go to a silly party at her house when she held out an invitation. There was my name—Tate Ellerbee, printed so pretty across the front of that envelope. I should have known it wasn't a genuine gesture when she didn't say, "Sure hope you can make it." But for about a zillionth of a second, I got a little excited. I even pictured me with a bunch of curls on my head, laughing with all the other girls. I guess V.C. caught a glimmer of that excitement on my face and couldn't wait to burst it. She said, "My momma said I had to ask you. She said you were the most pitiful thing with such a tragic life."

Hank Williams, you will be proud to know what I did next. I tore her invitation in half and slugged her in the gut. I should have put all of us out of our misery and aimed toward her vocal cords. It would've been a great improvement. Of course, I forgot that she is also a big tattletale. I ended up sitting in Principal Salter's office until Aunt Patty Cake arrived. She walked into his office, red faced, looking so hot that she could have melted a block of ice in Antarctica. Mr. Salter said, "I think washing every blackboard in the school would be a fair punishment." "More than fair," said Aunt Patty Cake. She folded her arms across her chest and tapped her foot against the linoleum.

There I was with a mop bucket filled with water and a rag in my hand, going from class to class. My arm got real sore, but I'm the kind of person who can find the upside in things. I decided to make up songs while I washed away numbers and letters. When I was finished,

Mr. Salter told me I wouldn't get off easy if it happened again. I wanted to ask him, What's the punishment for being a downright mean person? But I didn't.

I reckon V.C. knows I'm not going to be attending her back-to-school slumber party.

Rubbing my sore arm with
loads of BENGAY,
Tate P.

Dear Hank Williams,

SOME NIGHTS, I lie in bed and listen. The night carries
all kinds of sounds—an owl hooting, crickets chirping,
and frogs croaking. If I listen careful enough, I can hear
Momma singing "Oh, My Darling, Clementine." And
when Aunt Patty Cake begins to snore and Uncle Jolly
slips off to the Wigwam, I sing with Momma like we
did when she was here.

I've got a nice voice too (Momma told me she could
hear the big potential in my vocal cords). For some
strange reason, it's only when I'm here in my bed that
my voice comes out sweet and sorrowful like Momma's.
In front of other folks I get nervous, and it comes out like
a pig caught in a barbed-wire fence, squealing out the
high notes, croaking through the low ones. That's why I
hardly sing outside my bedroom. The last time I did was
when the youth from our church went caroling this past

Christmas. The choir leader asked me to stop belting the songs so loudly (which I believe was his way of letting me know my singing was not up to his standards).

But I'm determined to let my best shine through. I know I have talent, and when people have talent they should share it with the world. Just like you, Hank Williams. If only I could take voice lessons at Miss Mildred's Music Shop. Then I would be in top form for the Rippling Creek May Festival Talent Contest.

Miss Mildred wears cowgirl outfits like Dale Evans in the Roy Rogers movies—blouses with western yokes and skirts with white fringe. She owns enough cowboy boots to match every outfit. She buys bottles of Bouquet of Roses cologne by the dozens from Aunt Patty Cake, which explains why she smells like she's bathed in the stuff. I want to tell her that for a more subtle effect, she should lightly spray it in the air and walk underneath it, but Aunt Patty Cake won't let me. Miss Mildred teaches piano and voice when she isn't selling guitar picks or sheet music. Aunt Patty Cake takes me there every Tuesday after school for thirty minutes of piano.

Miss Mildred never teaches me a song worth singing.

Instead we practice scales with silly words like *Here we go up a road to a birthday party*. I believe music should fill up inside a person like air and make them think they're so light, they could float to the clouds. Hank Williams, that's the way you sound when you sing, like you're a part of those words coming out of your mouth, heading toward the sky. All practicing scales does is make my fingers ache. The whole time I'm thinking, I wish Miss Mildred would teach me voice lessons. Once, I asked her, "Miss Mildred, how about we use half my lessons for singing?" Do you know what she said? "Tate, some voices aren't meant to be heard." Well, I was fit to be tied!

Clearly, Verbia Calhoon has a voice that Miss Mildred thinks should be heard by the world. She thinks Verbia is going to be a big star, and so does Mrs. Calhoon. Mrs. Calhoon claims she is not only Verbia's mother but also her manager. That means she buys big stacks of songbooks for Verbia and arranges for her to sing solos in church every third Sunday. If I had all those voice lessons, I could do that. When my momma comes back from making that movie, she's going to see to it that I get the best voice teacher in the parish. We'll probably have to drive all the way to Alexandria, but Momma won't mind, because she knows I'm capable of singing like an angel too.

The songbird from
Rippling Creek,
Tate P.

September 13, 1948

## Dear Mr. Williams,

It's been a couple of weeks since I sent you my first letter. I'm wondering if you haven't answered any of my letters because I was disrespectful by using your first name. I reckon I forgot because they call you Hank Williams on the radio.

I should have written "Mr." in front of your name. Anyway, I didn't mean any disrespect. I want you to know my momma raised me right. Frog is a different story. Momma slipped up some on raising him.

Everyone has heard back from their pen pals, except for Wallace and me. (I doubt he wrote his cousin, because he said the whole pen pal idea was stupid.) Even Coolie and Theo Grace got letters all the way from Japan. You should have seen the red-and-purple stamps on their envelopes. They had pretty designs and funny symbols that Mrs. Kipler said were Japanese words. Theo Grace's pen pal drew a picture of a rabbit on the back of hers. The teeth looked so sharp. Coolie read his aloud, and everyone laughed when he got to the part where his pen pal asked if he knew Hopalong Cassidy. He's a big movie star. How would *we* personally know him? I'm sure my momma has met him, though.

This week, Mrs. Kipler said we should write about how we spend our day when we aren't in school. Did I tell you I was a cosmetics model? There ain't a woman around Rippling Creek that hasn't gotten a dab or dose of the Delightfully Devine Beauty Products that Aunt Patty Cake sells. Sometimes I ride with Aunt Patty Cake when she makes her calls. We start on the outskirts of Rippling Creek and wind our way through the backwoods until we meet the other side of town.

The only place Aunt Patty Cake doesn't drive to is Pine Bend, where the colored folks live. Once I asked her why. She looked annoyed and said, "I don't have to, because Constance gathers their orders and brings them to our house." That didn't really answer my question, but I can tell when Aunt Patty Cake is finished explaining. Besides, I think I know, anyway. Uncle Jolly says a white woman should never be caught going into Pine Bend. He makes it sound like there are murderers living there.

The other day Sudie Cartwright wanted to know what Tequila Sunrise Peach rouge would look like. Aunt Patty Cake rubbed two tiny dots on my cheeks. Mrs. Cartwright put on her glasses and came in so close to my face, her wiry eyebrows were inches from tickling me. She quickly straightened and said, "I'll take two pots."

When we drove away from the Cartwright house, I asked Aunt Patty Cake, "Why didn't you try Tequila Sunrise Peach on Mrs. Cartwright's cheeks?"

"Honey, did you see the rough condition of her skin? Reminds me of crepe paper. Sudie wouldn't have bought a single pot, but when she saw the rouge on your flawless cheeks she got caught up in the fairy tale."

"What fairy tale?" I asked.

"The fairy tale that maybe her fifty-seven-year-old cheeks could look as dewy fresh as your eleven-year-old ones. The beauty business is based on fairy tales, and every woman hopes they all come true."

So, see, Mr. Williams? I'm in the fairy-tale business too. Think of me as a fairy godmother without the wand. When we got home after making the rounds, Aunt Patty Cake went in the house, and I headed into the yard. Frog darted out from behind the magnolia tree next to the pasture fence. He's always hiding and trying to scare me. But instead of saying, "Boo!" he asks, "Whatcha got those pink dots on your cheeks for?"

Lord, I wish I had me a dog. If I had a dog, he would be loyal and true and wouldn't ask me a billion stupid questions.

The main reason I like to make the rounds with Aunt Patty Cake is so I don't have to be around my pesky little brother. At least his bicycle is out of commission and I don't have to worry about him trying to race that knucklehead Rudy in his convertible.

*Your fan and Delightfully*
*Devine Beauty Products model,*
*Tate P. Ellerbee*

PS—If I was a fairy godmother with a wand, I'd grant you three wishes. I'll bet your first wish would be to become the most famous singer in the world.

PPS—I like the song you sang on the *Louisiana Hayride* this week. Aunt Patty Cake still wonders what you look like.

Dear Mr. Williams,

THANK YOU FOR THE autographed picture! I was hoping
for a letter, too, but I ain't complaining. I'm probably
the first person in Rippling Creek who could recognize
you on the street. Aunt Patty Cake said, "I knew he'd be
pretty."

Uncle Jolly took a quick look at your photograph
and said, "Yeah, good thing he's a pretty boy, because he
can't sing." I probably shouldn't have told you what
Uncle Jolly said, but remember that comment came
from a man who ain't that pretty. Besides, Uncle Jolly
can't recognize talent the way I can. He only likes those
sad heartbreak songs.

Maybe someday you and Momma could sing in a
cowboy movie together like those Hopalong Cassidy or
Gene Autry movies. And you're a lot better looking than
Gene Autry. People would line up around the block to

see that show. Thank you again for the autographed picture. I'm mighty proud to have it, and now I have something to tell them at the post office when I mail another
letter if they go to snickering again.

Your fan,
Tate P.

PS—Aunt Patty Cake said we could hang your
picture over our Emerson radio.

September 15, 1948

Dear Mr. Williams,

A LOT OF FOLKS are going to the railroad crossing in town to wait for the Clyde Beatty Circus on its way to Alexandria. The circus will be riding the Missouri Pacific up from Opelousas and will reach our town around three thirty in the morning. Folks are going to get up in the middle of the night and wait along the tracks, hoping to catch a glimpse of an elephant's behind or a clown waving out the window. If you ask me, those folks are plain ole ridiculous. Seeing a blur of train cars rush by is nothing like sitting under a big top and watching a genuine circus.

Uncle Jolly is taking me and Frog to Friday night's performance. That's if Frog doesn't chicken out. He's afraid of clowns. Frog is always afraid of the things he shouldn't be and brave about the things that he should fear.

Anyway, let those crazy folks get up while it's pitch-dark and stand near the railroad crossing. I don't care if Verbia's mother is serving creamy hot chocolate to everyone like it's a big party. I'll be home sleeping sound in my bed, and when Aunt Patty Cake tells me to get up for school tomorrow morning I'm going to jump out of bed and say, "Ready for duty, ma'am!"

Sweet dreams,
Tate P.

September 18, 1948

Dear Mr. Williams,

THE CLYDE BEATTY CIRCUS was amazing! Just as I predicted, Frog wouldn't go. Yesterday afternoon when Uncle Jolly and me headed toward his truck, Frog took off and hid behind the magnolia tree. He had to stay and watch Aunt Patty Cake sack up her Delightfully Devine orders. At least I got out of that chore. Although I really don't mind helping her sort the products. It's fun to match up the lipsticks and rouges with the people who ordered them. Some of them select entirely the wrong color, but folks can be stubborn. And like Aunt Patty Cake says, "It's all a fairy tale anyway."

Back to the circus—it would have been perfect if Uncle Jolly's girlfriend, Dolores, hadn't come along. She is clearly not the circus type. She acted all uppity, making Uncle Jolly place napkins on the seat before she plopped down her big rear end. She kept fanning herself with her program and saying how the circus smelled like a chicken house. But after Uncle Jolly bought me some pink cotton candy and the music started playing, I forgot she was there.

When the elephants marched in, I couldn't help but think of my daddy and wonder if he ever took pictures of any in Africa. (Remember, he's a world-renowned photographer.) The elephants lined up straight as a row of dominos. The trainer raised his stick, and they stood on their hind legs. Dolores's face turned paper white when an elephant pooped ten feet away from us. Now, that was better than watching a blur of elephant butts racing by in train cars.

The tightrope was my very favorite part. This morning I gave it a try myself on the thick oak branch that stretches high above the ground. I held on to the branch above so I didn't fall, but someday I won't have to. Practice makes perfect. And in case you're curious, I'm still practicing my singing. I've decided I'll sing "Wildwood Flower" in the talent contest. When the Carter Family sings that on the radio, I can't get the song out of my mind. I find myself humming it all day long. Which reminds me—it's time to listen to you. The *Louisiana Hayride* will be on in fifteen minutes.

So long for now.

Your loyal fan and
oak-branch walker,
Tate P.

Dear Mr. Williams,

I'VE DECIDED TO BE my own voice coach until Momma comes home. Seeing those tightrope walkers and other brave circus performers reminded me that anything is possible. I almost forgot that. Don't *you* ever forget.

I've been practicing in front of the magnolia tree. Frog is my audience. He's always following me anyway. Figured I might as well give him something handy to do. Now I'll have to put up with him asking, "Whatcha gonna sing next?" At least Frog is an appreciative audience member.

No one knows I'm singing in the talent contest yet. Not even Momma, who I know would be proud. I want it to be a big surprise. I still have to practice my piano every day. We don't have a piano yet, but Momma has promised to buy us a baby grand first thing when she's finished with the movie. For now I go next door to

Mrs. Applebud's house. Mrs. Applebud is old enough to have a mess of grandchildren, but she doesn't have any, only a son who is serving in the military over in Japan. I reckon that's why she likes it when I come over to practice. She makes me peanut butter cookies. Frog doesn't eat any, though. In fact, he won't come in the house. He follows me to the door, then takes off. Some little kids are afraid of old people. I guess he's one of them. Every time I gobble down those cookies, I think, Frog doesn't know what he's missing.

You can bet Verbia Calhoon will enter the talent contest too, which means I've got to practice a lot. It's hard to beat a girl with perfect golden curls and big blue eyes. When she sings, people fall under a spell and get the false impression that she sings good. They are getting curls mixed up with singing on pitch. If Verbia sang on the radio, people would be turning the dial even if it meant they had to listen to static. And she would never, ever—not in a zillion years—be asked to sing on the *Louisiana Hayride*.

I'll be listening to *your* voice Saturday night. Maybe one day I'll sing good enough to be on the show with you. Won't that beat all?

Until then, I'll be singing for Frog at the magnolia tree.

Practicing to perfection,
Tate P.

PS—When Aunt Patty Cake saw me writing you, she asked, "Do you know how much stamps cost these days?" I don't think three cents is that much when it comes to friendship.

September 23, 1948

Dear Mr. Williams,

YOU HAVE A NEW FAN! When you sang "Lovesick Blues" the other night, Uncle Jolly dug out his handkerchief and blew his nose real hard before announcing, "That's the best dern song I ever did hear."

You might have gathered Uncle Jolly's girlfriend, Dolores, broke up with him last week. I didn't particularly care for her anyway. I don't know what Uncle Jolly saw in her. She was always telling him that he should do a hundred sit-ups every morning to get rid of his belly. Uncle Jolly can find someone better than her.

Back to that song—whoo-eee! That was something how you yodeled and sounded like you had a big ole sob in your throat waiting to come out. I wanted to learn that song, but there was so much whooping and hollering and clapping, I couldn't hear all the words.

I've got to run because Aunt Patty Cake and I need

to make some Delightfully Devine calls. She wants to win the contest they're having for the person who sells the most containers, by May 1, of their new face powder, Dream Dust. The winner of the Delightfully Devine Dream Dust Derby gets a weeklong trip to New York City!

Truth be told, Aunt Patty Cake doesn't seem like the type of person who'd want to go to New York City, but she is wearing out the tires on her car making her rounds. When the sample product came in last week, she took the soft pink pouf that comes with it and patted my face. Some of the dust flew up my nose, and I had a sneezing fit. "You need to hold your breath," Aunt Patty Cake said. Swear to sweet Sally, the things I do for this job!

Afterward I walked outside for some fresh air. Frog was sitting on the front porch swing. He was wearing those awful boots again. He took a glimpse of me, and his eyes nearly popped out of his head. Then he dashed off running. "You look like a ghost!" he yelled. I waited until he ducked behind the magnolia tree. Then I tiptoed over and hid, squatting on the other side of the trunk. After a while, he carefully peered around.

"Boo!" I shouted.

Boy, Frog sure can run!

Waiting by the radio,
Tate P.

PS—Please sing "Lovesick Blues" again. And again and again.

September 27, 1948

Dear Mr. Williams,

CONSTANCE WASHINGTON came over today to place a Delightfully Devine order for the Pine Bend folk. She drives to our house every few weeks so Aunt Patty Cake can write up the orders Constance has gathered. I asked Aunt Patty Cake if she wanted me to model the new products for Constance, but she only said, "No." I don't understand why, when she makes like my cosmetic modeling is such an important part of her business.

Constance has pretty skin—dark as a cup of Community Coffee—so she wouldn't be a candidate for the Devine Dream Dust Powder, but I think the Siren Red lipstick would be perfect on her. I told her that too. Constance said she might give it a try. Aunt Patty Cake told her she'd give her a tube if she wanted. She appreciates Constance's big orders.

Today Constance brought her daughter, Zion, with

her. She looked like she was ready for church, wearing a yellow dress and about a dozen tiny yellow bows in her black braids. Zion is eight, like Frog. But do you think he would stick around and play with her? Of course not. That meant I had to entertain her. While Aunt Patty Cake took Constance's order, I asked Zion, "Do you want to listen to me take my voice lessons?"

She nodded and followed me over to the magnolia tree. I was glad the tree was far enough away from the house that Aunt Patty Cake couldn't hear. I wasn't ready to tell her about my plans to sing at the talent contest.

Zion settled on the ground, resting her elbows on her knees and her chin in her hands.

All of a sudden I felt shy.

This was not like singing in front of Frog. This was someone I hardly knew. Did you feel that way when you sang on the *Louisiana Hayride* for the first time?

I took in a big breath, and then I started singing "Wildwood Flower." Zion sat there, not moving or smiling or frowning. I couldn't tell what the heck she thought of my talent. When I finished, she didn't clap or say a word.

"Well?" I said. "What did you think?"

"Did that song make your insides quiver?" she asked.

I told her, of course not. I wasn't a bit nervous.

"That's what I figured," she said. "You ain't singing from your heart."

"What do you know?"

"My daddy say when you really care about your singing, your insides quiver like there be butterflies flying around in your belly. My daddy knows. He be a good singer."

My cheeks burned. "Well, Frog likes my singing," I said.

"Frog?" She acted like she'd never heard of him. And I know she knows him. She'd been over here with her momma when I was practicing my piano lessons at Mrs. Applebud's.

"My little brother, Frog, remember him? He likes my singing just fine."

Her eyes grew wide. "You sing for Frog?"

"Yes," I said. "He'd be here this very minute, but he ran off when he saw the likes of you."

Then Zion's momma called out to her. She looked relieved to leave my voice lessons. No wonder Frog took off.

> Singing from my heart
> (always!),
> Tate P.

PS—I'm curious. Do your insides quiver when you sing on the *Louisiana Hayride*?

Dear Mr. Williams,

I GOT TWO ENVELOPES in the mail today. The first had another autographed picture of you. I don't know why you sent me a second photograph, but I sure do thank you just the same. If you don't mind, I'll send this picture to my momma, which brings me to the second envelope. I received a nice long letter from her. And oh, you should hear the things she's doing. She is very tired because it's hard to be a celebrity.

For instance, Momma begins her day before the sun comes up so she can exercise. (Actresses have to keep their slender figures.) She can't tell me about the movie yet because she's under contract to not talk about it. The movie people are worried folks would leak all the exciting parts. Then nobody would stand in line and pay for a ticket and a box of popcorn. They're probably right. If I told only one person and asked them to promise and keep a cross-their-heart-and-hope-to-die-stick-a-needle-in-their-eye secret, they probably wouldn't. Then they'd blab and blab so much about the movie, half of Louisiana would catch wind of it. And if Verbia Calhoon ever heard, Lord help us. If you don't want it told, don't tell Verbia. Her loose lips could sink ships.

Frog asked me to read Momma's letter three times. "When is Momma coming home?" he asked. "I miss her something bad."

Well, the way he said that made me wrap my arms around him and hug so tight until he said, "I can't breathe, Tate."

"I'm going to squeeze all that lonesomeness out of you," I said. When his face turned red as ripe tomatoes, I let go of him.

Then Frog fell back on the floor and burst into a giggle fit. I know how to get Frog's mind off the sad stuff.

Keeping my lips sealed,
Tate P.

October 3, 1948

Dear Mr. Williams,

TODAY WAS OUR CHURCH's annual Squirrel Gumbo Fundraiser. There is nothing better than a good bowl of squirrel gumbo to remind Rippling Creek that the air will soon have a nip to it. Aunt Patty Cake likes this time of year too, because her customers start ordering jars of rich cream to keep their skin from drying out. She says, "Nothing's better than Old Man Winter for the beauty business." I have a hunch Aunt Patty Cake prays for a cold front during the silent prayer time at Sunday Morning Worship services.

Frog likes this time of year too, because he loves baked yams. "They taste like candy," he claims.

I like baked yams too, but I'll take my candy with chocolate and peanuts, thank you very much. What is your favorite candy bar, Mr. Williams? If you write and tell me, I'll save up my money and buy you one. I figure you have to spend all your extra money on guitar picks and strings. But don't worry if you can't find time to write a thank-you note. I know you're awful busy.

Uncle Jolly says he heard that when you're not singing on the *Louisiana Hayride*, you're playing all over the state in high school gyms. I wish you'd come to Rapides Parish. A lot of singers perform at Bolton High School's auditorium in Alexandria. If you did come to Rapides Parish, I'll bet Uncle Jolly would take me to hear you. I reckon all that performing is why you haven't had time to answer any of my mail. You can still keep sending me pictures if you want. Only, can I have a different one next time? Maybe a photograph of you facing the opposite direction? That way I could hang it on the wall next to the other. Then, when folks stop by, I could tease them and say, "Did you know Hank Williams has an identical twin?"

I sent Momma the last picture you gave me, and she said all the women on the movie set thought you were a living dream. I hope that doesn't make you blush. But I wanted you to know that you have admirers all the way to Hollywood, California.

Although you haven't had time to write back, I hope

you don't mind if I keep writing. You've become a habit I just can't break. Hey, that sounds like the title of a song! You're welcome to use it, if you like.

Dreaming of a Baby Ruth
candy bar,
Tate P.

PS—If you do use my idea for a song, could you write at the top of the music sheet, "Title by Miss Tate P. Ellerbec"?

October 6, 1948

Dear Mr. Williams,

How COULD I HAVE BEEN writing all these letters without telling you what the initial "P" in my name stands for? I know you must be dying to know. The name is kind of embarrassing, but we've become close enough these last few months, it would seem a downright shame to keep it from you. Okay, get ready—the "P" stands for Pete. Are you done laughing yet?

There's a story behind that name. I'll tell you the short version. I am named after my daddy, who goes by Big Pete. When Momma gets mad at me, she calls me Little Pete. I prefer Tate P. myself or just plain Tate.

Sometimes when I'm not rehearsing my song, me and Frog play like we're spies for Governor Earl K. Long. If you are a spy, Rippling Creek is probably not the sort of place you'd want to be assigned. The most exciting thing that happens when we're spying is seeing Rudy

Branson speed by in his new convertible. His grand-mother left him a pile of money when she passed away.

For a while that was the talk of Rippling Creek. "What do you reckon Rudy is going to do with all that money?" Well, it didn't take Rudy long to hightail it to Baton Rouge and come back with a brand-new Chrysler Town and Country beige convertible. And ever since then, he can be seen speeding all over these parts. He drives it in the afternoon for his paper route and to show off.

When Rudy first started driving the convertible, Frog couldn't resist the chance to try and beat him. He'd wait on his bicycle at the end of our driveway, and when he heard Rudy's engine he'd place his right foot on the right pedal and rise on his toes on his left. When he heard Rudy approaching, Frog's back straightened. Seconds before Rudy reached him, Frog pushed off and started pedaling, his legs moving like windmill blades, his upper body leaning over the handlebars. Of course he never caught him, but Frog was determined to try. The first time he pushed off so hard that Big Pete's boot slipped off his left foot. He lost his focus, and he wobbled a few yards before falling on the road and scraping his leg.

I told him if he insisted on wearing those silly boots that were ten times too big, he'd better tie the laces. He never, ever listened to me. Now he can't race Rudy because his bicycle is nothing but a wad of metal from the close-call accident. (Frog is like a cat—he has nine lives.) And I don't care how much he begs, he ain't using mine. He'll have to be satisfied spying on Rudy from our yard when Rudy zooms by.

Usually the only folks we spy on are coming and going from the cemetery. Saturday after I was done practicing my piano lessons, Mrs. Applebud asked, again, if I would go with her on her cemetery walk. "No, ma'am," I said, "but I sure do thank you for asking." I should have known better than to practice this close to Mrs. Applebud's two o'clock visits.

I left, but I knew Mrs. Applebud would cut yellow mums from her yard, then head across the street. It takes her so long to cross that I worry she'll get hit by a car. My heart goes to thumping real hard when I see her take those tiny steps. Slump shouldered, she studies her feet, never checking to see if anyone is coming down the road. Somehow she always makes it to the other side.

So as you can see, being a spy for the governor is not all it's cracked up to be. If Frog hadn't wrecked his bicycle, we could pedal off and find some Reds to follow. But I don't much feel like doing it by myself, and Frog is too big to ride on my handlebars. Still, you never know what could happen across the street between burials and cemetery visits.

Your fan,
Agent RC Cola
(aka Tate P.)

October 11, 1948

Dear Mr. Williams,

I GUESS BY NOW you know the Cleveland Indians won the World Series. Uncle Jolly says he couldn't care less. "The day the Alexandria Aces make it into the World Series is the day I'll get excited," he says.

Silly Uncle Jolly. Doesn't he know minor-league baseball teams will never be in the World Series? Uncle Jolly rarely misses an Aces home game. When he has a girlfriend, he goes with her. When he doesn't, he sometimes takes Frog and me. Uncle Jolly carries his baseball glove because he's determined to catch a foul ball. Never has. Probably never will. But that's okay. At least he's trying.

I root for the Aces too, but one day I want to go to a World Series game. I've never been somewhere where there are tens of thousands of people. I figure it has to be exciting if all those people want to be in the same place. The only places I've been where there are a lot of people are the Clyde Beatty Circus and the Rippling Creek May Festival.

I'll bet the mention of the festival makes you curious how my personal voice lessons are going. Don't worry, I'm still practicing, practically every day. I need to be in top form for the talent contest. I must be getting better, because Frog used to put his hands over his ears when I reached the high parts, and now he doesn't do that. Although his left eye does squint a little, but I think that's a nervous tic that for some strange reason surfaces when I sing.

Your fan,
Tate P. (who is going to
a World Series one day)

PS—Did you know they played baseball in Japan? Coolie's pen pal, Keinosuke, is a big fan of the Osaka Tigers. We have the L.S.U. Tigers in Baton Rouge. Japan is more like us than I ever imagined.

October 18, 1948

Dear Mr. Williams,

I'VE MISSED PRACTICING my singing all week. I have the croup! The cough settled in my chest, and my voice comes out all crackly. When I speak, I sound like a bullfrog. Frog tries to make me talk just so he can laugh. Aunt Patty Cake quarantined me to my bedroom, but whenever she isn't nearby, Frog eases the door open and stands where only his right eye and nostril are visible. "Whatcha in bed for?" he asks for about the billionth time.

"I have the croup!" I croak, again.

Then, for about the zillionth time, Frog cracks up and slams the door. I can hear him giggling all the way down the hall and outside on the porch. Aunt Patty Cake never catches him, though.

The last couple of days, I've spent a lot of time staring out the window, not to spy but because I'm b-o-r-e-d. I've read both of my Nancy Drew books twice. There's nothing else to do. Yesterday at two o'clock, when Mrs. Applebud crossed the street to the cemetery, I tried to see if I could hold my breath until she reached the other side. I gave up because I was about to faint.

This morning there was a funeral for Arnold Fontenot, the barber. From my bed I could see and hear the doors of all the cars and trucks opening and closing across the street. Almost every man who lives in and around Rippling Creek went to Mr. Fontenot for their haircuts. They told him everything they knew, and sometimes he did the same. Uncle Jolly got in the habit of going to the barbershop whether he needed a haircut or not. He went to hear the gossip about what was going on around Rippling Creek.

Think of all the stories that got buried with Arnold Fontenot this morning. Although I'll bet he didn't take them all to the grave.

*Bored and suffering
mighty awful,
Tate P.*

October 19, 1948

Dear Mr. Williams,

It has only been a day since I wrote the last letter, but I thought I'd write you again (seeing as there's nothing else to do).

When I handed my letter to Aunt Patty Cake to mail yesterday, she asked, "You reckon he reads your letters?"

Her question made my blood boil, and nothing is worse than someone who has the croup and is mad, too. "Of course he does," I said. "He sent me two autographed pictures, didn't he?" I figured Aunt Patty Cake was adding up all those three-cent stamps in her head.

You do read my letters, don't you, Mr. Williams? I just wish I had a sign. I know I shouldn't have bragged about you sending me a picture, but I couldn't help but let it slip to Verbia Calhoon. It was third Sunday, the Sunday she sings her solo. Everybody made such a big deal about her off-key version of "Jesus Loves the Little Children," I had to deflate her a bit. People should not walk around with such a puffed-up idea of who they really are. But I should have known better than to let her air out, because she said, "Oh, those singers don't sign those pictures. They have a whole bunch of people who do that for them."

Sorry, but I couldn't think of anything to say except, "Well, he ain't *that* famous yet," which I do believe made her day.

But Aunt Patty Cake should know better than to doubt. She believes anything else like it's the God's truth. Even all those sad stories on *Queen for a Day*. Whoever has the most pitiful tales wins something wonderful like a washing machine. Every day when Uncle Jolly comes home from work, Aunt Patty Cake gives him the *Queen for a Day* report. "Today the lady who won told about how her house burned down. All her family owned were the clothes on their back."

"Who did she beat out?" Uncle Jolly asked, holding back a yawn.

"A woman whose husband left her."

Uncle Jolly was wide awake now. "Was she pretty?"

"What do you mean, was she pretty? I was listening to the radio."

"Did she sound pretty?"

Sitting in bed makes me do a lot of wishing.

I wish I didn't have the croup.

I wish Frog's bicycle wasn't messed up.

I wish my momma was done with that movie.

I wish Verbia Calhoon's blond hair would turn green.

Wishing and hoping,
Tate P.

October 26, 1948

Dear Mr. Williams,

I'M BECOMING AN EXPERT circus-goer. You might have thought the Clyde Beatty Circus beat all, but yesterday Uncle Jolly took me to the Greatest Show on Earth, the Ringling Bros. and Barnum & Bailey Circus. He picked me up from school early so that we could go to the matinee show. Verbia's momma picked her up early too. That's because she was sick with the croup. Poor pitiful Verbia.

Back to the circus—my brain is still dazzled by the sight of it all—fifty elephants, clowns, and the most incredible acrobats. Why, Rose Gold, the trapeze artist, swung right over my head! If I stood and stretched, I believe I could have touched her toes. When Emmett Kelly (he's that famous clown) circled the ring, I figured this is a clown Frog wouldn't be afraid of. Emmett's face is sweet and sorrowful, not at all scary.

Frog missed the circus again! This time *he* had the croup. And if you think I sounded funny when I was sick, you should hear Frog say "Whatcha" in his bullfrog voice. I saved some of my cotton candy for him, but when I offered it to him later, he just scrunched his face and shook his head. Remember, this is the boy who thinks yams taste like candy.

Across from where we sat I could see a group of orphans from the Masonic Home for Children. I wonder what it would be like to not have a momma and a daddy. Thank goodness I don't have to ever find that out.

Expert circus-goer,
Tate P.

PS—The circus had a long parade called the Night Before Christmas. Can you believe Christmas will be here in no time at all? And so will the Father and Daughter Potluck Banquet at our church. More about that next time. Or as they say on the radio—to be continued.

Dear Mr. Williams,

OF ALL THE ROTTEN LUCK! Dolores made up with Uncle Jolly. I should have known. He'd stopped singing that song by Sons of the Pioneers that goes, *You'll never know how I cried when I found out you'd lied.*

The next sign was when he woke up yesterday morning like it was Christmas and he replaced that sad song with "Blue Moon of Kentucky." He moved around our house like he was dancing a jig. Aunt Patty Cake asked him to slow it down. He was making our walls shake. Once, your picture fell and hit the radio. Uncle Jolly is not light on his feet. When Aunt Patty Cake told him to slow down, he grabbed hold of her hand and raised it high in the air. Then he twirled her underneath like she was a spinning top.

"James Irwin Poche, stop this silliness!" she yelled, but she didn't stop dancing.

When he went for another round, she let go and flopped back on the sofa, declaring, "Enough!"

Then Uncle Jolly grabbed my wrist and dragged me to the floor. It was fun, Uncle Jolly two-stepping me around the room with sweat glistening on his forehead and his belly bouncing like a bowl of Jell-O.

Anyway, I should have known Uncle Jolly and Dolores got back together by those signs. But no, I didn't realize what had happened until this morning. Uncle Jolly had promised to take me to see the new Donald O'Connor picture show at the Don Theatre in Alexandria. When we headed out of Rippling Creek, Uncle Jolly turned toward Glenmora instead of Alexandria. For a second I thought we might be going to the picture show in Glenmora, but before long we turned onto a dirt road that seemed to wind back into the woods forever. When we reached Dolores's house (which looks like the Big Bad Wolf could blow it down in a single puff), Uncle Jolly hopped out of his truck. "Wait here, Sweet Tater. I'll be right back." He sucked in his gut as he walked toward her front door. Purple-headed Dolores came out wearing a flowered dress and white gloves. How was she going to eat popcorn in those silly things?

Uncle Jolly opened the gate so that Miss Prissy could prance through. Then he asked me to step out of the truck to let her slide in next to him. A second later, I was jammed up against the window, inhaling Dolores's stinky perfume. The handle that rolls down the window was poking the side of my hip. That made it official, Dolores is a pain in the butt!

Miserable over Uncle Jolly's
choice in women,
Tate P.

PS—I can't believe I never asked you—do you have a girl?

*November 12, 1948*

*Dear Mr. Williams,*

Next Friday is the Father and Daughter Potluck Banquet at our church. Next to the May Festival Talent Contest, it is the most exciting time of the year. The daughters are supposed to make a favorite dish to share with the other fathers and daughters. I'm making a secret yam dish. Frog will be my taste tester since he's eaten about a million of them. I already know I'm going to have lots of butter and cane syrup in my dish. The cane syrup is the secret ingredient because when most folks think about sweetening yams, they think brown sugar. I'm not like most folks. And I want my secret yam dish to be a genuine true Louisiana dish. There'll be no store-bought butter in my special recipe. No sirree. The butter will be from Ebby Kizer's cow.

Here's how it happened: On a recent Delightfully Devine Beauty Products modeling assignment, I tried on Florida Sunrise Pink lipstick for Ebby. Now, Ebby doesn't fool like the other customers. She's on the plump side and has close-set eyes. The left one floats around as if it's scoping out the entire room. Her legs have bumpy trails that look like snakes under the skin. Aunt Patty Cake calls them the worst case of varicose veins she's ever seen. Still, after Constance Washington, Ebby is Aunt Patty Cake's best customer. "I do the best with what I've got," Ebby says (which I'm sorry to say isn't much).

Aunt Patty Cake calls Ebby's husband, Newman, an asset to her business. When I try on something that Ebby takes a notion to, she'll sample it herself. Then she goes in the next room, where Newman is doing his daily crossword puzzle.

"What do you think, Newman?" She pokes out her lips, turning them into a smooching pout.

Newman peers over his glasses and says, "Oh, honey. I wish you'd get some. In fact, you ought to get two tubes."

Aunt Patty Cake keeps applying more products on Ebby until she's about a layer short of looking like Emmett Kelly (remember the circus clown?). By the time we're done with our call, Aunt Patty Cake has made her biggest sale of the week. I reckon you can see why she checks to see if Newman's blue truck is parked outside before she calls on Ebby.

When I told Ebby about making a secret yam dish for the banquet, she said, "Well, then I think you need to have the best butter in Rapides Parish to go in that dish." If there was an entry for homemade butter at the Rapides Parish Fair, Ebby would win a blue ribbon. Ebby's cow, Mrytis, gives the best milk. Last summer the Kizers invited us over to eat some blackberry ice cream they'd made from it. So when Ebby offered me butter made from Mrytis's milk, I accepted wholeheartedly.

Yesterday I decided I needed one more ingredient for my secret yam dish. I let Frog decide if it should be cinnamon or vanilla. Frog said a little of both would do the trick. He also said my dish should have a good name, like the title of a song. I settled on Secret Agent Yam Mash. It sounded like something a spy for Governor Earl K. Long would make. Frog agreed.

You're probably wondering how I'm going to attend the Father and Daughter Potluck Banquet when my daddy is all the way over in Paris, France, taking pictures of the

Eiffel Tower. Well, Uncle Jolly, of course! He's not my daddy, but he will do in a pinch.

I can't wait until all those folks at church ask me what my secret ingredient is.

> Your fan and creator
> of the Secret Agent
> Yam Mash,
> Tate P.

PS—The night before the banquet, Aunt Patty Cake is going to roll my hair in rags. I'll bet I'll have more curls than Verbia.

November 16, 1948

Dear Mr. Williams,

THE OTHER DAY when I was rehearsing my song, I started wondering if you had a special lady. Then you go and sing with your missus. When they announced that Mrs. Hank Williams would be singing with you, it was as if you were reaching out of the radio to personally deliver my answer. After you finished that gospel duet, I said, "I'll bet Mrs. Williams is real pretty."

Uncle Jolly said, "Of course she is. I can tell by her voice." Uncle Jolly thinks if someone doesn't sing good on the radio then they must be good-looking. (Just a reminder—Uncle Jolly is no expert on singing.)

Do you have any children? If you do, is one of them a girl my age? If there was a Father and Daughter Potluck Banquet at your church, I'll bet you would take her even if it was on the night of the *Louisiana Hayride*. I don't know why, but I'm just certain you would. I feel as sure about that as Uncle Jolly feels sure about your wife being pretty. And if my daddy wasn't all the way over in Paris, France, he'd be taking me too.

*Sure of a lot of things,*
*Tate P.*

PS—I can't wait to tell you what everyone thinks of my Secret Agent Yam Mash and my curls.

Dear Mr. Williams,

WHY, OH WHY, did Dolores pick the day of the Father and Daughter Potluck Banquet to break up for good with Uncle Jolly?

Apparently she went and fell in love with a fellow named Chester Fairfield from Oakdale. Rumor has it, Uncle Jolly found out the hard way. He caught them zipping around Glenmora in Chester's new Chevrolet Fleetmaster. Now Uncle Jolly has the lovesick blues.

I guess he found all that out a few hours before I started dressing for the Father and Daughter Potluck Banquet. I was ready thirty minutes early. My Secret Agent Yam Mash was in Aunt Patty Cake's best bowl, wrapped with a warm towel. I was wearing my pink Sunday dress that Aunt Patty Cake bought for me at Penney's in Alexandria. And when she untied the rags in my hair, the curls came out somewhat tighter than I'd preferred, like a bunch of skinny mattress springs glued to my scalp. I'm not complaining. If anyone asks me about them, I'll just say it's the newest look from Hollywood.

Thirty minutes after the banquet was supposed to start, Aunt Patty Cake said, "We might as well eat. My mouth has been watering for that secret recipe of yours, Tate." But I told her no, maybe Uncle Jolly was just running late.

Frog and I settled on the porch steps. The moon was a great big buttermilk pie against the black sky. It stared down on me as if it was saying, "Still waiting?"

It was eight thirty before Uncle Jolly drove up. By then the banquet was halfway over. Remember I told you what else Uncle Jolly was addicted to? Well, it was clear he'd been at the Wigwam partaking in that addiction. He eased the car door open, but he lost hold of it. Then he leaned way over, trying to grab at the door to catch his fall. Lucky him, he caught it. He swung his legs out of the car and carefully stood. Still gripping the door, he hollered in a slurred voice, "I'll be ready directly, Sweet Tater." Then he rocked back and forth on his feet while he held on. Finally he straightened and swaggered toward the house.

Frog spit on the ground. That's how you know he's good and mad. I scooted over and let Uncle Jolly stumble up the steps. This time he forgot to open the door. He fell plumb through the screen and knocked the door off its hinges. Now it's good and broken.

Aunt Patty Cake rushed out to the porch, where Uncle Jolly lay facedown on top of the door. She opened her mouth a few times like she was going to give him a big ole speech, but all she managed was to shake her head and say, "Just leave him be."

She turned, and we followed her into the house, making giant steps over Uncle Jolly's body like he was a muddy rug we didn't want to wipe our feet on. Aunt Patty Cake set the table with sliced ham, leftover turnip greens, and my Secret Agent Yam Mash, but I didn't want to eat. I had a big hole inside me. Nothing could fill it. And here's the thing of it all—Uncle Jolly is not my daddy, and Big Pete might as well not be too.

When I was little, I would ask Aunt Patty Cake, "Was my daddy a bad man?"

"Now, baby, you have asked me that question a hundred times before."

"Well, maybe I need to know again," I'd say.

At breakfast, a while back, I asked Uncle Jolly about him. He told me, "Tate, your daddy wasn't a bad boy in the breaking-the-law sort of way. Let's just say he was a tomcat."

"But you never tell me what that means."

Aunt Patty Cake placed a plate of fried eggs and a slice of ham in front of me. "It meant he went a-creeping and a-crawling where he shouldn't have been."

"Is that why Momma ran him off?"

Aunt Patty Cake sighed. "Yes, ma'am, it is. Now stop asking your questions and eat."

Here is all I know about Big Pete:

– He is not a photographer, although he did leave behind a bunch of pictures he took when he and Momma went to Grand Isle on their honeymoon, and a pair of boots that I hate and Frog loves.

- He is not married to my momma anymore.
- He is not anywhere I know, and probably anywhere he wants me to know.
- The only thing I know about my daddy is his name, which he gave to me.

Sorry for the shameful lie,
Tate P. (which I wish
stood for Patricia)

PS—I'll tell you the real story about my momma tomorrow.

November 21, 1948

Dear Mr. Williams,

I KNOW YOU MUST THINK I'm the biggest liar in the great state of Louisiana, but Aunt Patty Cake told me to lock my lips about my parents' real lives. She says, "No use inviting trouble." Before I knew it, my little white lie grew and grew. Because Momma really is famous, and she did work in the picture-show business. But just not quite how I told it.

After Big Pete left, Momma started working at the concession stand, popping popcorn before the movies, dipping up ice cream cones after the shows ended. The way she tells it, Elroy Broussard the Third came to the Saturday matinee when a Gene Autry movie was playing. The movie had already started when Elroy arrived, but I guess he took one look at Momma and decided he wasn't in any hurry. Momma said she'd never seen a man dress so pretty. He spun a quarter on the counter and asked Momma, "Heads or tails?"

Momma said, "Heads."

Elroy tossed the quarter, caught it, and checked. "I'll be. Looks like you're going to an early dinner with me tonight."

Whenever Momma told that story, she ended it the same way. She looked up at the ceiling and shook her head. "It was like Elroy Broussard dropped plumb out of the sky and landed in front of me and the popcorn machine."

The first time Aunt Patty Cake heard it, she said, "Jordie June, you think the silliest moments are romantic."

To me, Momma is the most romantic person I know. Some people with good singing voices around here claim, "God gave me this gift," and they won't sing anywhere but church. Only church folk hear them Sunday after Sunday.

Momma wanted to share her gift with the world. She drove all around Rapides Parish with Lulu Swenson, singing in places where people could hear her. Aunt Patty Cake never said anything, although the way her mouth twitched every time Momma went, I could tell she didn't like it. Every Friday and Saturday night, Momma grabbed her purse, headed out the front door, and slipped into Lulu's car. Lulu's and Momma's voices harmonized like sisters. Which some say makes the best harmony. But personally I think a mother and daughter do.

I know because Momma and I sang together late at night when she'd get back. She'd try to be real quiet so as not to wake me, but I was always waiting to see the headlights of Lulu's car pull up in front of our house. I kept my window cracked just in case I fell asleep. When I heard Momma say "good night" in her hushed tone, my eyes popped wide open.

The front door squeaked and then our bedroom door. While Momma changed into her nightgown, I stayed quiet. After she slipped into bed, I'd whisper, "Momma, let's sing."

She'd sigh. I knew she was bone-tired, but she always asked, "What are we going to sing, Tate?"

"'Keep On the Sunny Side,'" I'd say, or "'My Darling, Clementine.'"

Momma would start out singing soft so that she

didn't wake Aunt Patty Cake. Her voice moved through the lyrics as if she was on a big stage. Like someone sticking their toe in the water, I'd join in the middle. Singing with her made me feel like I'd hitched a ride on a cloud. We'd finish with Momma saying all dreamlike, "Thank you, very much." Then she'd fall sound asleep. That's what I miss most about her. Lying in the dark, side by side, singing together, oh so sweetly, until Momma found her way to dreamland.

I don't know why Mr. Broussard came all the way from Crowley to the Glenmora picture show. I wish he wouldn't have. The first time he came around here, Uncle Jolly said he looked like a gangster with his fancy suit, shiny shoes, and tilted hat. He gave Aunt Patty Cake a bouquet of roses, Frog a slingshot, and me a Little Orphan Annie doll.

Frog immediately ran to find a rock outside and practice. Me, I don't play with dolls. Never have. But I said thank you just the same because I saw Momma giving me her three-two-one look. That's her countdown look, meaning if she had to start counting, I would be in trouble by the time she reached "one."

So I said, "Thank you, Mr. Broussard. You shouldn't have, sir."

Momma smiled and winked at me.

They left in Mr. Broussard's black Mercury. Aunt Patty Cake, Uncle Jolly, Frog, and I stared as the car rode past the Applebuds' place and disappeared around the bend.

"Highfalutin nonsense," said Uncle Jolly. Then he spit on the grass. (I guess Frog gets that nasty habit from him.) Aunt Patty Cake didn't say anything, so I followed her into the house and said, "Those sure are nice roses."

She was filling a vase with water. "Mm-hm" was all she said.

"I'll bet Mr. Broussard is rich."

She turned toward me with raised eyebrows. "Why do you say that?"

"He bought all this stuff for us."

She turned back to the sink. "Could be."

That was as far as I could get her to go on the subject. Aunt Patty Cake loved to give her opinions, but when she didn't want to, her lips could be as tight as Dolores's girdle squeezed over her lumpy rear end.

Momma went out with Mr. Broussard almost every night. But Mr. Broussard stopped coming around our house. I don't think he liked how Uncle Jolly gave him the three-two-one look. Instead Mr. Broussard picked Momma up at the picture show, and she didn't get in until late. She stopped singing. The only reason we know was because a couple of weeks later, Lulu drove up and said, "Tell your momma that I wish she'd let me know if she doesn't want to sing together anymore. Mr. Lacombe is threatening to replace us if she doesn't come back."

Momma got fired from the picture show in Glenmora. For weeks, she'd called in sick and gone on dates with Mr. Broussard instead. And since she wasn't singing with Lulu anymore, she wasn't making any money.

She used to talk about getting a big break and being discovered like Lana Turner at a drugstore soda fountain. But now she seemed to be more interested in Mr. Broussard's big break.

"What is it that man does all day besides strutting around like a proud rooster?" Uncle Jolly asked.

"He's a businessman," Momma said.

Uncle Jolly snorted. "I reckon I know what kind of business he's in."

Momma rolled her eyes and left the room.

"What kind?" I asked Uncle Jolly.

"The no-good kind."

Nobody around here seemed to explain things where I could understand. Aunt Patty Cake with her talking about Daddy's tomcat ways, and Uncle Jolly with his griping about Mr. Broussard's no-good kind of business. A person could go crazy dreaming up things about what that means. That day, I thought I'd never know what Mr. Broussard's no-good business was. But then, two weeks later, I found out. And oh, how I wish Momma had never seen the likes of him.

Mr. Williams, this sad story has plumb worn me out. I'll finish telling you about Momma tomorrow.

> In a sleepy and sorry
> state of mind,
> Tate P.

Dear Mr. Williams,

BRACE YOURSELF FOR a dramatic ending to Momma's story. One day Momma had been gone longer than usual. We heard from Mrs. Ronner before the sheriff called us. That's how fast news travels in Rippling Creek. Mrs. Ronner's son's best friend's cousin works at a Shreveport bank. His bank got a call because a Texas bank near the Louisiana state line had just been robbed. After holding up the bank, the man ran out to a car that was being driven by a young woman. The driver took off fast and lost control. The car hit a fire hydrant, and water spewed everywhere. Momma never could drive good. The car backed up quickly and didn't stop until it hit the front door of the bank. By that time, I imagine, the alarm was going off.

Momma got five years. That was thirteen months ago. I will be fifteen years old when Momma gets out of prison. I'll have all kinds of things happen to me that she'll miss. And she has already missed a lot.

A few months after Momma arrived at the women's prison in Huntsville, Mr. Goree, the prison warden, heard Momma singing. He plucked her up and set her down right smack in a women-prisoners singing group.

You see, Mr. Williams, my momma is a Goree Girl. Not anybody can be a Goree Girl. You have to have committed a murder or stolen someone's money or maybe driven a car during a bank robbery like Momma did. You also have to have a voice like a honky-tonk angel so that you can sing on the radio. Momma lives at the women's prison in Huntsville, Texas. She is Number 000851. But when she is a Goree Girl, everyone calls her Pretty Miss Jordie June from Rippling Creek, Louisiana.

They sing at fancy parties, the prison rodeo, and on the radio. That's how they got known all over Texas. Some folks outside Texas know about them too because their radios can pick up stations from far away. Since Shreveport is near Texas, maybe you've heard of them.

Some nights I sneak out of bed and turn the dial trying to pick up a Texas station that's playing the Goree Girls. But the furthest station I ever reached was out of

New Orleans, and that's in the opposite direction. So I lie in bed and listen for Momma's voice, and when the wind carries it to me, I sing along.

Now you know the real story about my momma, Miss Jordie June Ellerbee. I'm sorry that I have told such big stories about my momma and daddy. I'll understand if you never want to hear from me again.

Hoping Mr. Hank Williams
will forgive me,
Tate P.

PS—The part about Momma's friends saying you were a living dream is true, only it was the Goree Girls who said it. That's what Momma wrote in her postcard.

November 26, 1948

Dear Mr. Williams,

HAVE YOU FORGIVEN ME YET?

Hopeful,
Tate P.

*November 29, 1948*

Dear Mr. Williams,

THANK YOU for another autographed picture of you! I knew it was your way of saying you'd forgiven me. On Thanksgiving Day, I prayed your heart would soften toward me. And Saturday while listening to you on the *Louisiana Hayride*, I hoped you might send me a sign of some sort. Then today here came that envelope with your photograph.

Don't worry. I'll never mislead you ever again. I'm a forgiving person too. I forgave Uncle Jolly for messing up the night of the Father and Daughter Potluck Banquet at Rippling Creek Southern Baptist Church. Uncle Jolly felt awful bad about it. In fact, here's a special news report: Uncle Jolly hasn't had a drop of whiskey since! And no, it's not because he has a girlfriend (he doesn't). Aunt Patty Cake says sometimes people have to hit rock bottom before they can start climbing up.

After Uncle Jolly's hangover went away, he drove to the hardware store in Lecompte and bought some screen to fix the porch door. He fixed it good and painted it. He asked me to choose the color.

"Pink," I said, just out of meanness for what he'd done. I guess he knew why I said that, because then he apologized and asked how he could make it up to me.

Most people would say, "That's okay. I'm glad you're walking on the right path now." But I'm not like most people. I told Uncle Jolly flat out, "I want to hear my momma sing on the radio."

"Tate, we'd have to go all the way over to Texas to hear her."

Aunt Patty Cake overheard. She stepped into the living room and kept drying the bowl while she spoke. "James Irwin Poche, you are not going to Texas. Bad things happen to this family in Texas." She wasn't only meaning about Momma getting arrested. She was also talking about my grandma and grandpa.

Aunt Patty Cake was still drying the bowl even though there wasn't a drop of water on it. "No sirree. You are not going to Texas." With that said, she walked back into the kitchen.

Uncle Jolly looked at me all shy like, but I didn't back down. I set my jaw in a way that meant business. Finally he said, "Let me think on it some."

I believe good things are waiting around the corner for me—performing in the May Festival Talent Contest and hearing my momma on the radio. Until then, Mr. Williams, I'll listen to you.

Grateful that Mr. Williams
is the forgiving sort,
Tate P.

PS—In case you're wondering, Uncle Jolly painted the screen door green. Now our house makes you think of Christmas all year long.

December 3, 1948

Dear Mr. Williams,

I WANT YOU TO KNOW that I have kept my promise to not share our correspondence (except for the pictures you sent me). Of course, I realize that's probably why you haven't sent me a real letter. Every time you sing, you're getting a little more famous, and famous people can't be talking and writing about their lives. They have to be private. One exception is Momma, who loves being a celebrity. The only problem is, I can't talk about her because Aunt Patty Cake thinks it's best that nobody is reminded about where Momma is. Then when she gets out of prison, it will be easier for her to get back to normal.

I know you don't have enough time to write a long letter, but have you ever thought about sending me a postcard? That's what Momma does. Momma's so busy with her singing and other duties, she hardly has time to write a long letter. But every few days, we can count on receiving a postcard. I could paper the walls in my bedroom with her postcards. Instead I tie them with ribbons and keep them in a cigar box. If you wrote on the back of a postcard, you'd only have to write a sentence or two, like Momma. It wouldn't take too much time, and I would treasure it forever.

If I did stick Momma's postcards on my wall, I'd hang them where the backs showed. Then I'd have Momma's words surrounding me—*Don't forget to brush your hair a hundred strokes every night. Mind Aunt Patty Cake all the time and Uncle Jolly some of the time. Say your prayers and say one for Frog and me. Do you ever think about going anywhere out of Louisiana? Let's go to Paris when I get out.*

I wouldn't mind just going to a World Series game. But I'll go to Paris or anywhere else in the world with Momma when she gets out. Aunt Patty Cake wishes Momma wouldn't write on the back of postcards. "Everyone around here knows Jordie June's business." Personally, I'll take a postcard or a long letter from her. Frog feels the same way, although it always makes him sad when I read them. I think he forgets about her being gone until we receive one. Sometimes I think he's mad at her for leaving us.

Theo Grace and Coolie are the only kids who share their pen pal letters. How could those other letters compare with the ones from the Japanese kids? They tell us all the things they eat, which may sound like that would be boring, but it's not. They seem to like rice as much as us, but they also eat raw fish. They call it *sushi* and *sashimi*. Of course Wallace had to blurt out, "We call that bait here." Everyone ignored him because we were too busy listening to Theo Grace read about how they pull their shoes off at the door and sleep on mattresses that fold called *futons*.

All that stuff is interesting, but nothing could compare with having Mr. Hank Williams as a pen pal.

> Luckier than I deserve to be,
> Tate P.

PS—Now you know three Japanese words— *sushi*, *sashimi*, and *futon*. I guess I'm the next best thing to having an international pen pal.

December 5, 1948

Dear Mr. Williams,

YESTERDAY UNCLE JOLLY took Frog and me to see *The Count of Monte Cristo* in Alexandria. His truck was in the shop, but Aunt Patty Cake let us take her car. After the show he drove by City Hall, which was lit up like Mrs. Applebud's birthday cake. The building was covered in thousands of lights. Every corner has a huge sparkling Christmas tree and lights spell MERRY CHRISTMAS over each entrance. Just the sight of it all plopped me smack into the Christmas spirit. Even Frog was speechless.

On the way home, Uncle Jolly drove over to Hoyt Home Appliances in Lecompte. When we pulled up, the store went dark. We'd arrived right at closing. Frog had fallen asleep on the way over there, but Uncle Jolly and I hopped out to get a closer look at the Victrola in the window. Not only could it play phonographs, it also had an AM/FM radio. We were in such a trance, it took us a second to see the salesgirl waving at us from the front window. By the time we did, she'd moved away from the window and opened the front door.

"You want a closer look?" she asked. She was tiny, with black hair and blue eyes, and appeared to be about Momma's age.

Uncle Jolly didn't answer her. He seemed too busy taking in her beauty. I glanced at the lady's wedding band on her left hand. Sure enough, someone else had noticed her beauty before Uncle Jolly. He was always sizing up the wrong woman.

I nudged him in the side with my elbow.

Uncle Jolly blinked, but his mouth still hung open. I was afraid he'd start drooling.

"Uncle Jolly, the lady asked if we want to go inside."

He stammered. "Uh, uh, uh, no . . . that's okay, ma'am. You're closing and all."

I was glad Uncle Jolly didn't say yes. Frog could wake up and think we'd abandoned him.

The saleslady came outside and joined us in front of the window. "It comes in mahogany or walnut. Which would you like?"

"Ma-ma-ma-hog-gany," Uncle Jolly said.

I had to step in before he bought a Victrola he couldn't afford. "How much does that Victrola cost?"

The lady pointed to the sign at the foot of the Victrola that somehow we'd missed. Now I could see it as clear as day—$209.50!

Uncle Jolly snapped out of his trance.

"That includes fifty phonographs," the saleslady said.

Mr. Williams, you'll be happy to know what my next question was. I asked, "Are any of them by Hank Williams?"

"I don't believe we have any of those yet."

"Then we wouldn't be interested, would we, Uncle Jolly?"

"Well, now . . ."

The lady laughed. "I never lost a sale over Hank Williams before. I guess we better look into getting some of his phonographs. Which song do you like best?"

" 'Move It On Over,' but Uncle Jolly likes 'Lovesick Blues.' "

"That's my favorite too," she said, smiling at Uncle Jolly.

"That a fact?" Uncle Jolly leaned against the wall and

tipped his hat. That lady knew how to sell a Victrola to Uncle Jolly. He was settling in. I had to think quick.

"Uncle Jolly, we better go. Frog will be waking up and wonder where we're at."

Uncle Jolly turned toward me like I'd snapped him with a rubber band. For a few seconds, he didn't say anything, just stood staring at me. Then he looked to the lady and said, "I'll come back when it isn't closing time."

"If you do, I wish you'd ask for me. My name is Garnett."

"Garnett," Uncle Jolly said, "like the jewel. My name is James Poche."

I'd never heard Uncle Jolly introduce himself with his real name.

Garnett held out her hand. "Nice to meet you, James."

Uncle Jolly went to reach for Garnett's hand, but I grabbed his sleeve and tugged.

"Come on, Uncle Jolly. Remember Frog?"

Uncle Jolly glared at me but pulled the keys out of his pocket. He smiled at Garnett, tipping his hat. "Thank you, ma'am. I'll check back soon."

"And what's your name, young lady?" she asked.

"Tate," I said, walking away fast. "Maybe we'll be back when you get those Hank Williams phonographs." See, Mr. Williams? I'm doing what I can to shoot your fame all the way to the moon.

Back in the car, Uncle Jolly started the engine and asked, "Tate, why'd you tell her Frog was asleep?"

"I didn't. I said he might wake up." I glanced back at Frog stretched out on the back seat. Big Pete's boots had slipped off his feet and I could see his toe sticking out of a hole in his sock.

Uncle Jolly's eyes grew soft. Then he shook his head and looked straight ahead at the road. He didn't talk to me the entire drive back. His mind seemed elsewhere as he stared ahead while we moved down Highway 112. A few times I heard him whisper under his breath, "Garnett like the jewel."

Here we go again.

Your fan and public
relations person,
Tate P.

Dear Mr. Williams,

WHEN I SAW ZION and her mother walking up our driveway yesterday, I told Frog, "Come on! Let's hide!" Frog, who runs faster than Superman, took off around the back of the house. I'm not so quick, so I slipped behind the barbecue smoker Uncle Jolly built. I had to squat behind it, since the smoker is only about three feet high.

My thighs burned from squatting so long, but when I heard the screen porch door slam shut, I thought I was safe and stood.

"Hi!" Zion said.

She caught me.

Zion was wearing a blue plaid coat. It looked like she got it from the Wellan's Department Store, but I knew she didn't, because that would cost a lot of money. "Are you hiding from me?" she asked.

Now, I almost said no but quickly changed my mind.

Besides, how else would I explain why I was squatting behind a barbecue smoker? So I said, "Frog and me were playing hide-and-seek."

"Can I play?" she asked.

We played for the next twenty minutes. I wish Frog hadn't left. I think he would have liked playing too. We got hot and sweaty, playing so hard. I threw off my jacket, and Zion unbuttoned her coat. She didn't take it off, though. I think she was proud of it, because she told me her momma made the coat from leftover fabric she had after sewing Mrs. Calhoon's curtains. I sure would hate to match anything in Verbia's house.

Later, when it was time for her to go, Zion joined her momma on the driveway. She turned and cupped her hands around her mouth. "Tell your brother I said hello."

Mr. Williams, you wouldn't believe what happened next. Her momma gave her a good slap on the behind. Zion rubbed at the spot all the way to the car. My momma would never have popped me for hollering out to someone. Zion was only being friendly.

Aunt Patty Cake didn't see what happened because she was already in the house, going on and on about how Constance placed her biggest Christmas order. I didn't tell her what she did to Zion, but I did tell Frog. He asked, "Whatcha think her momma did that for?"

I said I had no earthly idea but that he should have come back sooner. In a way, what happened to Zion was his fault.

*Never staying hid for long,*
*Tate P.*

PS—I've started my New Year's resolution early. I am now practicing my song for the talent show every single day, no matter how cold it is outside. I'm a professional like you and Momma. I show up and sing.

December 15, 1948

Dear Mr. Williams,

COOLIE'S PEN PAL, Keinosuke, sent him a samurai sword guard. That's a fancy piece of metal with a slot where the sword goes through. Coolie stood in front of our class holding it up. "Now imagine," he said, "that I'm a real samurai and I've got a long samurai sword that would go through this guard when I wore it."

Those were the most words strung together Coolie had ever said in class. He is the shortest boy in sixth grade and is usually quiet, but not today. Keinosuke had turned him into a samurai. Wallace seemed impressed too. I could tell by the way he was leaning forward over his desk and trying to take a good look at that samurai sword guard. Then he mouthed off and said, "I'll bet one of our soldiers has the sword after he used it on Keinosuke's dad."

Mr. Williams, you will not believe what happened next. Little shy Coolie charged across the room toward Wallace. He held the holder out as if it was a sword. When Coolie reached Wallace, he pushed him back. Wallace lost his balance and fell to the floor. The desk turned over, making such a clatter. Then the students closest to the action pushed their desks away and spun them around with their feet so they could have a front-row view. The rest of us ran over and formed a circle on the outside. It was more exciting than listening to Billy Fox and Jake LaMotta box on the radio, because this fight was happening right in front of our eyes.

Coolie straddled Wallace's belly and took turns punching each cheek, one with his fist, the other with the holder. "That's my friend you're talking about," Coolie yelled.

Mrs. Kipler rushed over and pulled Coolie off Wallace. She grabbed hold of the back of both boys' collars and dragged them to the principal's office. Big ole Wallace's face was bleeding, but he was yelling, "He didn't hurt me!" the whole way.

Mr. Williams, if someone ever said something that

mean about you, I'd curl up my fists and fight in your honor. I wonder what Keinosuke would think if he knew sending that samurai sword guard started World War III in our class today.

Ready to defend your honor,
Tate P.

December 20, 1948

## Dear Mr. Williams,

I HOPE YOU AND MRS. WILLIAMS are enjoying your first Louisiana Christmas. With Momma and Uncle Jolly away, it's quiet around here. You already know where Momma is, but Uncle Jolly has gone to Dallas, Texas, with a load of Christmas trees. He won't be back home until after Christmas. Aunt Patty Cake, as you can probably imagine, is not happy about that. The trees come from Jeter Hopkins's land. Jeter told Uncle Jolly that if he would haul them over to Texas and sell them, he'd split the money. Mr. Hopkins had heard there was big money in Dallas and that it was amazing what those city folks would pay for a pine tree.

Our Christmas tree has dozens of stories on it. We have a tradition in our family where we pull an ornament off the tree each night for the ten nights leading up to Christmas. Each of the ornaments is homemade and represents a story.

Last night, we were stringing popcorn for the tree when I pulled off the moon-shaped blue satin one. Aunt Patty Cake sighed when I handed the ornament to her. In a flat tone, she said, "That was made from the dress I wore the night I met a boy at a fais do-do in Ville Platte." In case you don't know, Mr. Williams, a fais do-do is a Cajun dance party.

She handed it back to me as she pushed her eyeglasses into place and returned to pulling the needle through a popped kernel.

"Well?" I asked. "Is that all?"

"Afraid so."

I wasn't going to let the story stop there. Aunt Patty Cake had always been just Aunt Patty Cake to me. Kind of like a grandmother. I couldn't picture her as a girl.

Aunt Patty Cake shrugged. "Not much to tell. There was a fais do-do at my cousin Callie's house. All the furniture had been removed from the front rooms of their house in order to make room for dancing."

I'd seen that around Rippling Creek, too. Last week, we passed the Colfaxes' house, where they had such a big dance that even the beds were in the yard. Folks were dancing on the porch. Mr. Williams, have you ever played at anyone's home? When I'm sixteen, I plan to have a big birthday party. Maybe you could play at it? If you keep your schedule that far in advance, that will be March 12, 1953.

My thoughts returned to Aunt Patty Cake's story when I heard her tapping her foot to the music on the radio. "Did you dance?" I asked her.

"Of course I danced. My daddy was French." She said it as if Cajuns popped into life doing the two-step.

"You only dance when Uncle Jolly is goofy and spins you around the floor."

"He hardly gives me a chance to object. When I get good and ready to dance, I will."

"So you were good and ready back then?"

She looked up at me, but I knew my question kept her at that fais do-do in Ville Platte. Then she gazed across the room and smiled. "He was a good-looking boy."

"As good-looking as Hank Williams?" I asked.

"Better!" she said.

Now, Mr. Williams, remember this is Aunt Patty Cake, who was only married for about half a minute and probably never, ever had a kiss. And she has to wear glasses to see anything three inches in front of her face.

Aunt Patty Cake studied the wall, smiling, as if she was looking out at the fais do-do in Ville Platte. "The house was so crowded with couples bumping into each other as they shimmied across the floor, he suggested we dance outside."

"Was he a good dancer?" I asked.

"He was French."

"Guess that explains it, then."

"All the songs were upbeat, and we were twirling around the furniture so fast, I kept wishing for a slower tune to catch my breath."

I'll bet breathing wasn't the only reason Aunt Patty Cake wanted a slow tune. Slow songs meant you held each other close.

She continued. "Then, finally, the fiddle player played a waltz. But it was a short dance. The clouds had rolled in and let loose of the rain. Even though the music stopped, he wouldn't quit dancing. He held on to me, and we glided around the couches and chairs as the rain poured down on us. When the men rushed out to rescue the furniture, he still wouldn't let go of me." Aunt Patty Cake chuckled and shook her head.

"Guess he was breathless too," I said, but Aunt Patty Cake didn't hear me.

"I haven't thought about that dance in years."

"What happened next?" I asked her.

"The rain ruined my blue satin dress. It was never the same."

"I meant what happened with you and the boy."

"I never heard hide nor hair of him again."

"Why don't you ask someone about him?"

Aunt Patty Cake raised her left eyebrow. "Why don't you go sweep the kitchen floor?"

Frog is smart. He never is the least bit interested in the Christmas-tree-ornament stories. Curious people seem to have more chores. Once, I had to scrub this house from top to bottom when I asked Aunt Patty Cake about an old picture of her and a man. Later, Momma told me it was Aunt Patty Cake's wedding picture. Back then, I didn't know Aunt Patty Cake had been married.

"Only for about two months," Momma had said.

"Then they divorced. She keeps the picture to remind herself of her bad judgment in selecting men." That's something Momma, Uncle Jolly, and Aunt Patty Cake all seem to have in common—their pitiful partner picking. I sure hope Frog and me don't suffer from the same affliction.

Still, the ending of Aunt Patty Cake's fais do-do story was the saddest I ever did hear. And it didn't have to be. She could find out what happened to that boy. I don't understand folks that could have a happy-ever-after ending but have no gumption to try. I can tell you're not that way, Mr. Williams. You're living an exciting life, and in no time at all the whole world will know the name Hank Williams.

Hope you and the Mrs. have a Christmas tree filled with happy ornament stories.

Holiday wishes from
your #1 fan,
Tate P.

PS—Be on the lookout for a Christmas card with glittery stars all over the envelope. It's from me.

*Christmas Night, 1948*

**Dear Mr. Williams,**

You'll probably receive the Christmas card I sent yesterday the same day you receive this letter. That's why I wrote *Read this letter second!* on the back of the envelope. I couldn't wait to write you because of all the good news.

First, we received a Christmas card from Momma. Inside she wrote, *Wishing my family a Merry Christmas filled with love! And I'm sending an extra hug to Tate! Ask her to write me, please. Love and kisses, Jordie June.* (She forgot to mention Frog, and I know that hurt him something awful. But Momma can be the forgetful type.) She wrote, *PS—The Goree Girls are going to sing at the warden's house for Christmas Eve, and we'll get to eat all kinds of delicious food, but I know none of those dishes will beat Aunt Patty Cake's Holiday Maple Sugarcoated Ham with Pineapple Rings.*

Momma hopes being a Goree Girl will help her get

out of prison quicker. A lot of fans of former Goree Girls wrote letters to the judge, begging him to let them out early. Some of them did get released sooner. The judge called their singing an act of good behavior. Momma is the most popular Goree Girl, so I expect her fans will write a bunch of letters.

Aunt Patty Cake thinks I should write one. But here's what I think—if the judge knew that my pretty momma had two children she seemed to forget about when she drove the getaway car, I think the judge might make Momma serve more time. He'd think she must not be a very good momma if she put a man like Elroy Broussard before her children. Right now, everything looks like it could go Momma's way—her singing for the Goree Girls, making all sorts of people so happy that they write letters on her behalf. No reason to unravel all the good things they are doing with a letter from me. It's funny how Aunt Patty Cake wants me to write a letter for Momma but she acts like she's ashamed of Momma being a Goree Girl. Imagine that. Her own niece is famous, and she won't mention it to anyone.

Back to what else happened tonight—Mrs. Applebud came over for dinner. It was nice to have her sitting at our table, since Momma and Uncle Jolly couldn't be there. Mrs. Applebud brought a platter of deviled eggs with paprika sprinkled over their whipped yolks. The way those eggs melted on my tongue, I could have gobbled down a dozen of them.

Of course Frog headed for the Vicks VapoRub at the first whiff of Mrs. Applebud's deviled eggs. Thank goodness Aunt Patty Cake baked yams and biscuits, too.

Mrs. Applebud had some news. Her son got married last week to a Japanese lady named Yuki. I asked, "Do they eat *sushi* and *sashimi*?"

"I'm not certain, dear," Mrs. Applebud said. "Why don't you find out? She has a ten-year-old daughter named Keiko. You could be her pen pal. That would help her learn English."

"I already have a pen pal," I told her. "I'm writing Mr. Hank Williams."

Aunt Patty Cake probably thinks I didn't hear her sigh, but I did. (If you could just write me one letter, she could see what good pals we are.) But I was afraid I might have sounded rude to Mrs. Applebud. So I quickly said, "I guess this means you're a grandmother."

Mrs. Applebud's smile lit up her face. "Yes, it does.

It's the best Christmas present ever. And it will be official as soon as Albert can adopt her." Then she pulled a picture out of her purse. Albert was in his navy uniform next to Yuki, a lady with the creamiest skin I ever did see. Keiko, her daughter, was holding a Shirley Temple doll.

I wonder what Wallace would think about Mrs. Applebud's news. It's probably a good idea they live over in Japan, because judging by the response to Mrs. Kipler's offer for Japanese pen pals, I think they might feel unwelcome here.

After dinner Aunt Patty Cake turned on the radio to KALB, and we listened to Christmas music. She'd started to cut the pecan pie when who do you reckon drove up? It was Uncle Jolly! All the way back, safe and sound, from Texas.

Aunt Patty Cake sighed long and hard. I guess she was relieved that someone finally broke the Texas curse on our family.

"Ho, ho, ho!" he yelled from the screened porch.

And then I heard a whimper. It sounded like it came from a dog. I sprung from my chair and beat Frog to the door.

When I opened it, Uncle Jolly stood there holding a Louisiana Catahoula cur. Most folks around here call it a cur dog. She was full grown but as sweet as a puppy. Her hair was spotted like a leopard with a big dose of white that spread from her belly all the way up to her neck, and on the tip of her tail, which pointed toward the sky. Her icy-blue eyes reminded me of Frog's marbles.

"Is she ours?" I asked, locking my hands together. I was falling in love fast and I couldn't bear to touch her if she was going to the pound or to someone else's family.

Uncle Jolly offered her to me. "She's all yours, Sweet Tater."

My hands parted and made their way clear to that dog. I held her next to me as close as I could, and if I was the type of person who cried (which I'm not), I would have cried a mountain of happy tears. She lowered her head, but I could tell she liked me. She didn't wiggle to get out of my arms.

"Thank you, Uncle Jolly! This is the best Christmas present ever." I glanced over to Aunt Patty Cake, remembering her no-dogs rule. She was smiling too.

Uncle Jolly rubbed the top of the dog's head. "You'll let me have some squirrel-hunting rights with her, won't you?"

"Yes, sir."

Uncle Jolly took off his coat. "Cur dogs are some of the best hunting dogs."

The dog licked my fingers like she was cleaning me real good. Aunt Patty Cake and Mrs. Applebud came over for a closer look.

"She's pretty for a cur dog," Aunt Patty Cake said. "Of course she'll have to be an outdoor dog."

I guess she saw my disappointment, because she quickly added, "She can stay inside until bedtime tonight. Only because it's Christmas."

A slow grin traveled across Uncle Jolly's face. "Sissy, you are a softie."

"Wouldn't want that to get around," Aunt Patty Cake said, making her way back to clearing the table.

Uncle Jolly dug in his pocket and pulled out a piece of torn newspaper. "There's one more gift, but we'll have to wait until after Christmas to get it. Remember this?"

He held out the scrap of newspaper, and I recognized

the Victrola we saw in Hoyt's window in Lecompte. "I'll bet we'll be able to hear your momma on that beauty."

Aunt Patty Cake's face turned red. She glimpsed at Mrs. Applebud, but she was petting my dog.

"What are you going to name her?" Mrs. Applebud asked.

"Lovie," I said. I couldn't begin to tell you how I thought of it, but as soon as the name left my lips, I knew it was the perfect fit.

The grown-ups started talking about Texas, and I got bored. I reckon you could say I enjoyed being the center of attention. Frog had been real quiet, and I searched around the room for him. He was hiding behind Aunt Patty Cake's chair, his arms wrapped around his body as tight as thread on a spool. Like I told you before, Frog is afraid of the things he shouldn't be and too brave about the things he should fear. But this time Frog didn't look afraid. He looked sad.

I held Lovie out to him and whispered, "She can be yours, too, Frog." Well, it was like his body unfolded right in front of me. His shoulders let down and his arms relaxed. He stretched his fingers toward Lovie's head.

While he petted her, I scratched her back. Lovie took right to it. This dog is going to be spoiled rotten if Frog and me have anything to do with it.

Merry Christmas again!

Your fan and new dog owner,
Tate P.

December 26, 1948

Dear Mr. Williams,

AUNT PATTY CAKE said Lovie has to sleep outside in the
shed. The shed is not a place where anyone should have
to sleep. It's dark, filled with old junk coated with thick
cobwebs. But I didn't argue, because I knew the only
way Aunt Patty Cake would ever allow me to keep Lovie
was if I kept her out of the house. So last night after
Mrs. Applebud left, I carried Lovie out to the shed. Uncle
Jolly went with me to help find a good place. He started
searching around for some old saddle blankets we'd had
from the days when Uncle Jolly owned a horse. While
Uncle Jolly hunted for them on the high shelves, I combed
the lower ones. That's when I came across my daddy's
boots. I was glad they weren't on Frog's feet, but the
sight of them made me freeze.

Uncle Jolly must have noticed, because he came over

and grabbed them. "Meant to throw those out," he said. "Good time as any."

Frog wouldn't like it. "They're magic," he'd tell me. He'd stand tall, looking down, admiring those boots. I think Frog believed if he wore them enough, our daddy would appear in front of us in his socks. I was glad Uncle Jolly was throwing them out. Frog didn't need to be wearing them anyway. They were way too big for Frog's little feet. He could trip or fall or worse.

When Uncle Jolly returned, he patted me on the shoulder and went back to scouting for the blankets. A moment later he said, "Here's one." He handed me the blanket. I held it by two corners and flapped it into the air a few times. Dust flew, causing us to cough. Then I folded it and placed it on the dirt floor. I patted Lovie's new bed and looked up at her. "Come on, girl."

Lovie studied me and the blanket. Then she slowly made her way to the spot. I raised my hand to pet her head, but she ducked away as if I was going to hit her.

Uncle Jolly shook his head. "Poor thing. I think she

was running away from some downright mean scoundrel. They must have mistreated her something awful. Haven't heard her bark once."

"Where did you find her?" I asked. I wanted to know Lovie's whole story.

Then Uncle Jolly told me how he discovered Lovie. He was heading back from Dallas. He said he was so happy with his pocket filled with Christmas-tree money because he knew now he'd be able to buy the Victrola and we'd get to hear Momma on the radio. "I was thinking to myself, this must be what Santa Claus feels like, knowing he's going to please all those boys and girls by getting them something they really want. Anyway, I was driving on Highway 80 and it began to rain, hitting the windshield so hard, I could hardly see. Hate to admit it, but I got scared all of a sudden."

"But it rains here all the time, Uncle Jolly."

"Yes, ma'am, but I was in Texas. And your aunt Patty Cake's words kept playing in my head. I was afraid I was going to meet my maker right outside Mineola. I decided not to push my luck. I pulled over to the side of the road, practically driving into the woods because of what happened to your grandparents. As soon as I parked, I knew I'd done the right thing. At least that's what I thought until lightning struck a huge limb that landed about two feet in front of my truck. Talk about a close call.

"Then I heard a yelp. I could tell it was from a dog, and normally I would have stayed put, but something got me curious, maybe because I only heard the sound once. I buttoned up my coat and fixed my hat on my head and stepped out into the rain. Then I checked all around the truck, but I didn't see anything. I figured whatever it was had taken off. When I headed back, though, I saw a dog's tail with a tip of white on the end sticking out from underneath the truck. I fetched my leftover ham sandwich and coaxed her to come to me. She was shaking, but I sweet-talked her. Finally, she inched her way out from underneath and let me lift her inside the truck. I figured we'd wait the weather out together, but by the time the rain stopped falling I'd come to the conclusion that this dog was meant for someone special."

"Thank you, Uncle Jolly."

"Yeah, I was thinking this dog should go to my next

girlfriend," Uncle Jolly said. He looked dead serious. Then he winked.

Mr. Williams, did I ever tell you that Uncle Jolly thinks he's funny?

Until next time,
Tate

*December 29, 1948*

*Dear Mr. Williams,*

THERE ARE TWO WINDOWS in my bedroom. One faces out front where I can see the cemetery across the road. The other gives a view of the shed in the side yard. I hardly ever looked out the side window, but now that Lovie has to stay in the shed at night, I have good reason to be staring out that window. Christmas night it was so hard to go to sleep, knowing poor Lovie, who'd prob-ably never had much love before, was sleeping out there by her lonesome. She didn't make a sound, but Uncle Jolly said he'd never heard her bark at all.

The next night, my mind fretted on it so much, I couldn't sleep. Mr. Williams, you know me by now. I'm the sort of person who makes the best of situations. Aunt Patty Cake said Lovie had to be an outside dog. But Aunt Patty Cake would want me to get a good night's sleep.

So I was in a dilemma. On one hand, I could leave

Lovie out in the shed and toss and turn all night. Or on the other, I could respect Aunt Patty Cake's strict rule about getting a good night's sleep. I weighed each option very carefully and realized Aunt Patty Cake would know if I didn't get enough shut-eye, but she'd never know if Lovie became a part-time inside dog. (And if you want to get picky about it, a shed is inside too.)

That decided, I threw back the covers and eased my window open. I tiptoed to the shed to get my dog. Good thing I'm a part-time spy.

Now, Lovie is not a small dog. She's not a big dog either, but that night she seemed heavier than when Uncle Jolly handed her to me for the first time. Lovie was a willing partner. She stayed quiet and didn't yelp when I accidentally dropped her onto my bedroom floor. I quickly climbed in after her and shut the window.

Most dogs would have headed straight to that bed, but not Lovie. She stood watching me, waiting to see what I was going to do next. I crawled into bed and patted the foot of the mattress. Lovie cowered like I was going to swat her. Swear to sweet Sally, I know someone hurt this dog bad. I waited and tapped the bed again. She glanced away. Then she checked back. I kept patting the bed, whispering, "Come on up, girl." Finally, as if she realized that I was absolutely serious about my offer, she hopped onto the foot of my bed and curled into a tight ball.

I wish I could have told Frog, but he would have let the cat out of the bag. That boy gets too excited about some things.

I know my secret is safe with you, though.

*All my best,*
*Tate and Lovie, too*

PS—I'd better start setting my alarm a few minutes earlier so I can sneak Lovie back to the shed before Aunt Patty Cake heads to the kitchen.

Dear Mr. Williams,

HAPPY NEW YEAR! I believe 1949 is going to be a great
year for you and me. It's already off to a terrific start
because I have Lovie. This year I'll be singing at the
Rippling Creek May Festival Talent Contest, and I believe,
with all my heart, this year you'll become a household
name around the entire United States. You're already a
big star in Rippling Creek. Aunt Patty Cake listens to you
every morning at 7:15 sharp. She even bought Johnnie
Fair Syrup the other day at the Piggly Wiggly just because
you sang about it.

This is also the year we will hear Momma on a Texas
radio station. The other day Uncle Jolly went to Hoyt's,
and the Victrola was not the only thing he walked out
with. He lined up a date with Garnett. I know what
you're thinking. There is that wedding band on her left
ring finger. IMPORTANT NEWS FLASH: Garnett is a

war widow! Well, I've never been so happy about someone being dead in my whole life. Garnett wears the ring
to steer off unwanted advances. I guess Uncle Jolly isn't
on that list, because the next time I saw her, she wasn't
wearing it.

Uncle Jolly took her to dinner at Herbie K's in
Alexandria. He told Aunt Patty Cake and me all about
it. "You should see her eat," he said. "I've never been on
a date where a woman cleans her plate. I don't know
where Garnett puts it. She's as tiny as a thimble."

I get to witness the next date. Uncle Jolly invited me
to go to the movies with them. "Garnett said you could
be our chaperone," he told me.

I'll report back all about it in my next letter!

Your fan in 1949 and hereafter,
Tate P.

January 8, 1949

Dear Mr. Williams,

GARNETT IS NOTHING LIKE DOLORES or any other of
Uncle Jolly's past women. She is bubbly and thinks life
is a big bowl of strawberry ice cream! At the picture
show we saw a Roy Rogers movie. When the bad guy
showed up, Garnett threw popcorn at the screen and
yelled, "Boo!"

I knew Uncle Jolly was embarrassed, the way he
glanced around. But then folks all around us joined in.
Popcorn flew over the seats, and chants of "boo" came
from row to row. Frog and me joined in. Then, lo and
behold, Uncle Jolly tossed a big handful at the screen.
Uncle Jolly should never plan on becoming a baseball
pitcher. The popcorn landed in a lady's hair. She turned
around and scowled at us, but I never had such a good
time at a picture show.

Aunt Patty Cake likes Garnett too. She likes anyone

who likes her food and tells her so. Especially people who don't act as if they wish they could spread a layer of Vicks VapoRub underneath their nostrils.

I hope Garnett doesn't ever break up with Uncle Jolly. He hasn't sipped anything stronger than Community Coffee since the Father and Daughter Potluck Banquet. I'm afraid if someone as special as Garnett broke up with him, he'd fall off the saddle for good. He's so relaxed around her. He never sucks in his gut. He just lets his belly hang over his belt. Garnett must think it's cute, because she sometimes rubs his tummy, closes her eyes, and says, "I'm making a wish."

Everyone likes Garnett. Lovie likes her because she brings her Ritz crackers tucked in her coat pocket. I know Frog likes her, because he's real bashful but he doesn't run off like he did with Uncle Jolly's other girls.

Aunt Patty Cake wrote and told Momma about her, and she wrote back saying, "It's about time Jolly got smart. Tell him she's a keeper."

I've been practicing my song in front of the magnolia tree. Lovie seems to like "Wildwood Flower" just fine, but Frog says he wishes I'd choose "You Are My Sunshine" instead. I still haven't told my family I'm planning on singing in the talent contest. I want the timing to be perfect before I spring it on them.

Bye for now.

Your fan,
Tate P.

January 14, 1949

Dear Mr. Williams,

OUR SECRET HAS BEEN DISCOVERED. Aunt Patty Cake caught Lovie on my bed early this morning. When I heard the door squeak open, I almost sprang up, but it was dark. I decided to pretend I was asleep and pray she didn't see Lovie. The door closed, and then it quickly opened again. I squeezed my eyes shut so tight, I could feel them quiver. Aunt Patty Cake let out a long sigh, then slowly closed the door.

My heart pounded. I threw back the sheets and jumped out of bed. Then I eased the window open and stepped through to the outside. When I patted the windowsill, Lovie came over and rested her front paws on it like I trained her. (Mr. Williams, this is a smart dog!) My hands surrounded her rib cage, and I gently lifted her out of the room. My next plan is to teach her to jump outside by herself when the alarm clock sounds.

After I got her settled inside the shed, I returned to my room the way I'd left. I scanned every inch of the floor. Lovie hadn't had an accident. Then I walked into the kitchen. Aunt Patty Cake was sitting at the table drinking her coffee and reading the paper. Uncle Jolly was pouring himself a cup from the aluminum drip pot on the stove. I yawned real big, locking my hands and stretching my arms up to the ceiling.

I was thinking, Boy, am I lucky. That had been a close call.

Without looking up, Aunt Patty Cake said, "Guess you'd better put my old wedding-ring quilt on the floor if Lovie's going to stay in your room at night."

Uncle Jolly took a big swig of coffee, but I could see his smirk. I felt the blood leave my face. Just when I think Aunt Patty Cake is as predictable as the sun rising, she goes and surprises me. Well, even the sun goes out for an eclipse sometimes. And with no husband, Aunt Patty Cake sure didn't need a wedding-ring quilt.

> Owner of a part-time
> inside dog,
> Tate P.

Dear Mr. Williams,

CONSTANCE CAME TO OUR HOUSE to place an order today, but Zion wasn't with her. Frog and me were sad about that. I wanted to sing my song for her. I've been practicing every spare minute. I don't know why it's so important that I convince a little kid I'm a good singer and know how to sing from my heart. Lovie wags her tail when I sing. I figure that's a dog's way of clapping.

There are other things I've learned about a dog. I'll share them with you, in case you ever consider getting one.

1. A dog will follow you around like a best friend. Better than a best friend, because she will love you no matter what (even if you yell at her for peeing on the bed).
2. A dog probably shouldn't sleep on your bed because she might forget she is a dog. (That

fact comes from Aunt Patty Cake. She said that after Lovie peed on mine.)

3. Dogs are like goats. They will eat almost anything, including lipstick (the reason Lovie is on Aunt Patty Cake's three-two-one list), so feed them food that is good for them or they'll get fat like Abner Hill's hound, who waddles like a duck.

4. A dog pours a pitcher of love into the lonesome spots of your life. Not that I have many of those. I'm a busy person.

*The Dog Expert of Rippling Creek,*
*Tate P.*

February 3, 1949

Dear Mr. Williams,

LAST WEEK, Uncle Jolly wrote Momma and asked her to let us know where she'd be singing. Every day I check the mailbox as soon as I get off the school bus to see if she's sent a letter or postcard. Every day I'm disappointed. Frog acts like he doesn't care, but Lovie comes with me and waits patiently.

Uncle Jolly took Lovie squirrel hunting the other day. I hoped she would make Uncle Jolly proud. After all, he saved her from a terrible home life. All morning I paced around the house.

"Have you got ants in your pants?" Aunt Patty Cake asked me.

I looked out the window so many times, Frog gave up pestering me. Finally I saw Uncle Jolly and Lovie at the road. Uncle Jolly had a rope tied to Lovie. I grabbed my coat and ran out of the house.

Lovie wagged her tail when she saw me. Halfway up the driveway, I noticed Uncle Jolly didn't have any squirrels. "Uncle Jolly, how'd she do?"

Uncle Jolly shook his head. "Tate, Lovie is no squirrel dog. Beats me. She's a pure cur. Anyone can see that, but she doesn't have any interest in squirrels. Heck, three darted right in front of us, and she didn't even turn in their direction."

Well, I have to admit, I was disappointed myself. "Why did you tie a rope around her?"

"She kept running off. At first I chased after her, figuring she found some bigger game. Maybe squirrels weren't enough challenge for her. When I caught up, I found her under a shrub slapping crickets."

"I guess Lovie likes hunting bugs." Maybe squirrels bored her. I started to think about all the things that bore me—collard greens, long sermons, and hearing Verbia Calhoon sing. Then I completely understood. A person can't love everything on God's green earth. Why should a dog?

Uncle Jolly walked up the porch steps, shaking his head. "Beats all I ever seen. A cur dog that don't like to hunt."

I untied the rope and gave Lovie a good scratching on her back. She rolled over so I could reach her belly. I gently raked my fingernails up and down her. Then I found her tickle spot. The sight of her left hind leg digging in the air was so funny.

Lovie may not be much at hunting squirrels, but she's real talented at making me smile.

Hoping life is treating you
real good too,
Tate P.

February 12, 1949

Dear Mr. Williams,

I HAVE THREE important things to tell you.

First, Garnett brought me a present today—it was your new record with "Lovesick Blues" on it! She said it had just come out. I asked if I was the first person in Rapides Parish or at least Lecompte who owned it. But Garnett is an honest person, and she said, "I wish you were, Tate, but by noon that day we'd sold every copy. We'd only bought a dozen. But we've ordered more." (See? I told you, Mr. Williams. Your fame keeps spreading.)

Second, Momma finally sent us her performance schedule. Uncle Jolly and I've been turning the dial each night, scouting the Texas radio stations on her list. We keep a Big Chief paper tablet next to it and write down every time we discover one. Unfortunately Momma wasn't performing on any of the stations we'd found. Then today we received a postcard from Momma that said the Goree Girls would be singing on WBAP in Fort Worth. And guess what? WBAP *is* on our Texas radio station list! In a couple of weeks, we'll be listening to Momma on the radio. Uncle Jolly kept his promise!

The third thing I want to tell you is that that very night is when I plan to tell Aunt Patty Cake and Uncle Jolly I'm going to enter the talent contest. I can't wait to see their faces!

> Fan of the almost-very-
> famous Mr. Hank Williams,
> Tate P.

PS—I forgot—I have *four* important things to share. Theo Grace's and Coolie's pen pals said that Japan has Children's Day the same week as our May Festival. People will be celebrating all around the world!

February 19, 1949

Dear Mr. Williams,

YESTERDAY I CAME HOME from school all excited about what Mrs. Kipler had learned about Children's Day in Japan. They wear kimonos, and the boys' families hang huge carp streamers outside their doors. The streamers represent a story about a carp that was so strong, he swam upstream and became a dragon. I couldn't wait to tell Frog. He'll probably wish he had a carp streamer.

When I got off the bus in front of our house, I expected to see Lovie waiting for me at the mailbox. Come rain or shine, she is always there. She heads to that spot each afternoon. A few minutes later Aunt Patty Cake hears the moan of my school bus stopping at our driveway. Aunt Patty Cake says Lovie is better than a clock. The first time I saw Lovie sitting there, it nearly melted my heart. Before stepping off, I turned and told the entire bus, "That's my dog."

But today I couldn't find Lovie anywhere. She wasn't near the magnolia tree, in my room, under my bed, in the shed. She was nowhere to be found. Aunt Patty Cake said, "Tate, she's a dog and she knows who feeds her."

Right when I was thinking of jumping on my bike to go out and find her, Mr. Rockfire drove up in his truck.

Mr. Rockfire stuck his hand out the open window and waved. Then he stopped the truck in front of me. My hands squeezed the handlebars. I didn't have time to talk.

"Think I have something you might want," he said. At that very minute guess who stood on all fours in the truck bed? That's right! Lovie!

"I think your dog and mine are sweet on each other," Mr. Rockfire said. Corky was a cur dog too. His coat was gray with specks of black. He wore the proud title of being best squirrel-hunting dog in Rippling Creek.

Aunt Patty Cake came out of the house. The sun was shining so bright, she rested her hand over her eyebrows so that she could see. "Gayle? Not used to seeing you this time of day."

Then she noticed Lovie. "I see you found her. Well,

you certainly made Tate's day. Come in this house. I'll put a pot of coffee on."

Mr. Rockfire opened the truck door and stepped out. "Only if it's no trouble."

Aunt Patty Cake wiped her hands on her apron. "No trouble at all."

While Mr. Rockfire followed Aunt Patty Cake into the house, I hugged Lovie, and she wagged her tail like she was happy to see me. I hadn't thought of Lovie as the romantic type.

> Never planning on being
> sweet on anyone,
> Tate P.

February 23, 1949

Dear Mr. Williams,

VERBIA CALHOON BRAGGED and bragged today about
how her momma booked her at the Central Louisiana
Junior Livestock Show in Alexandria this weekend.
When I told Frog and Lovie, we had a good laugh over
the thought of Verbia singing to a bunch of calves and
hogs. Nothing against the people who go there, but
that gives me another reason not to join 4-H or Future
Farmers of America.

I should have let that image satisfy me enough, but
when Verbia bragged about it for the eighteenth time, I
ignored Aunt Patty Cake's advice to not discuss Momma's
situation. I said, "That ain't nothing. My momma is a
Goree Girl. She's singing on the radio in Fort Worth
Thursday night."

Do you know what she said? "Your momma is doing
time in a Texas prison."

My hands curled into fists, and it was all I could do not to hit her. But then I thought about the Rippling Creek May Festival Talent Contest, and I didn't go any further. If I had boxed her chin or yanked her curls, Miss Mildred would have kicked me out of the talent contest for sure. And as much as I hate to admit it, Verbia was right. Momma was serving time.

The other day I rode my bike to the post office to mail my letter to you. Mr. Snyder asked, "Is that another letter to Mr. Hank Williams?" (Which I do believe is none of his business.) Two older girls from my school, Clara Banks and Evelyn Milton, swung around like they'd caught me stealing something.

Mr. Snyder snickered. "You got company. They're fans too."

"We listen to Hank Williams every Saturday night," Clara said, as if she'd discovered you all by herself.

Evelyn nodded. "We only missed it twice, and that's because we were visiting my aunt Mertie in Pineville. She doesn't like listening to the radio. She says music gives her a headache."

"I'll have you know, I got three pictures from Mr.

Hank Williams," I told Mr. Snyder, hoping the girls would hear.

Do you know what they said? Well, I guess you do know. They said, "We have three too."

I don't know why that made me jealous. It might sound silly, but I thought I was the only one writing to you. All the way home I pedaled with a heavy feeling inside me. I'm not proud to admit it, Mr. Williams, but I was kind of mad at you. Then I realized that what I, Tate P. Ellerbee, had predicted back in the summer was happening. You *are* famous!

> Your #1 fan of all
> your fans,
> Tate P.

PS—Two more days until I get to hear Momma sing on the radio and make my big announcement. Don't worry, I may be busy, but I'll still be tuning in to the *Louisiana Hayride*. And so will Aunt Patty Cake (who never gets a headache listening to you).

Dear Mr. Williams,

HAVE YOU EVER HAD a night that started out being what you thought would be the best night and then something happened and it ended up becoming one of the worst nights instead?

That's what happened last night. We were all gathered around the new Victrola. Uncle Jolly set the dial to WBAP, the Fort Worth station where Momma and the other Goree Girls would sing. It was coming in as crisp and clear as a Louisiana winter day. Uncle Jolly had invited Garnett, who was every bit as excited as me. Aunt Patty Cake surprised us by pulling her own chair over close enough to hear.

My heart pounded when I heard the announcer say, "Now here's the Goree All Girl String Band performing 'Will the Circle Be Unbroken.'" I could hear Momma's voice singing lead as it drifted from the speaker so loud and pure. It was as if she was standing smack in our living room singing.

When Momma sang the solo part of the next song, Uncle Jolly turned to Garnett and whispered, "That's Jordie June."

Garnett smiled and mouthed "Oh my!"

"That's my momma," I told Lovie. Frog was quiet, hugging his legs, and I could see how he was feeling like me. He missed Momma real bad.

After the Goree Girls finished, Garnett began to clap. Then we all did. Uncle Jolly flipped off the radio. "Hard to top that."

Everyone wore a happy glow, the kind you get when something wonderful has happened. I remember thinking, *This* is the perfect time. I stood up. "I can't top it, but I've got some good news to share."

Right off, Garnett leaned forward like she couldn't wait to hear. "What's that?" she asked.

"I'm entering the singing category of the Rippling Creek May Festival Talent Contest."

Well, you would have thought I'd let the air out of everyone's tires. Everyone except Frog and Garnett, who slapped her knees and said, "Tate, that *is* wonderful news!"

But looking at Aunt Patty Cake's and Uncle Jolly's faces, it didn't seem so wonderful to them.

Garnett didn't let me down. "I'll bet you have your momma's gift. Why didn't you tell me that, Jolly?"

Uncle Jolly stammered, "Well . . . I . . . well, I . . . just don't know." Little beads of sweat spotted his forehead.

Aunt Patty Cake leaned forward. "Are you certain you're up for that, Tate?" Why didn't she say what she was thinking? "You can't sing, Tate. Not like your momma."

Garnett started to fill in all the miserable holes Aunt Patty Cake and Uncle Jolly were shooting in that happiest day. She kept talking about how delightful it was and how she could take off work and maybe she could get a front-row seat and she could borrow her friend Mabel's camera and take a picture of me. But it made no difference. Nothing she said stirred Uncle Jolly or Aunt Patty Cake to her way of thinking. I didn't bother telling them I'd been practicing for months. I'd rehearsed so much, Frog was probably tired of hearing me. After I went to bed that night, Frog sneaked into my room and tiptoed over to my bedside. "I think you sing real good," he whispered. "I like 'You Are My Sunshine' the best."

That was not the song I was planning on singing in the talent contest, but I knew he was trying to make me feel better. I reached out to squeeze his hand, but he rushed away before I could catch it. And even though my little brother thinks I'm a good singer, my head was crowded with Aunt Patty Cake and Uncle Jolly's reaction when they'd heard the news.

And that, Mr. Williams, is how the best night ever became the worst.

In a sorry state of mind,
Tate P.

March 2, 1949

Dear Mr. Williams,

AFTER MY BIG ANNOUNCEMENT, Aunt Patty Cake made me practice the piano every single day except Sunday. She was hoping to change my mind about entering the singing part. More than a few times, she said, "You might think about playing a song on the piano, Tate. That's where you have the most experience."

The only song I could play on the piano was "Twinkle, Twinkle, Little Star," and I was not going to let Verbia Calhoon have the satisfaction of hearing me play that in front of the audience. It doesn't matter how you jazz up that song, it still sounds like a silly kiddy tune. But I keep Aunt Patty Cake happy by showing up at Mrs. Applebud's every day after school and playing those stupid scales.

And almost every day Mrs. Applebud says to me, "I could wait and go over to the cemetery later in the day, if you would want to go with me." And when she says that, I say, "No, ma'am. Thank you, kindly." I don't have plans to take up cemetery walking as a hobby.

Mr. Williams, I've learned that just because some folks don't believe in me doesn't mean I should stop believing in myself. And I'm not alone. She's never heard my singing, but Garnett believes in me, and so do Frog and Lovie, and they've heard me.

Rest assured, I'm still singing at the talent show.

Living on the sunny side
despite all opposition,
Tate P.

Dear Mr. Williams,

FROG AND ME got so excited about seeing Zion with her momma coming up our driveway. We waved, but when she started toward us, her momma said, "Remember what I told you."

Zion said, "Yes, ma'am," then walked slowly over to us.

"Frog and me were wondering when you would come back," I told her. She looked scared. Then I realized Lovie was with us and she'd never seen her.

"This is Lovie." I showed her how to hold out her palm and let Lovie smell her good.

Lovie sniffed at her hand and licked her knuckles. Well, Zion practically melted into a puddle. Her fear seemed to disappear, and her face broke into a big grin. That warmed up my insides. I like when people like my dog.

"Do you want to hear my song again? I've been practicing a lot."

She nodded, and I told her to sit right next to Frog.

She kept standing.

"I don't want to sit next to him," she said.

"Suit yourself," I said, but I could tell Frog was sad about it.

Zion settled across from him. Lovie left Frog's side and settled down by Zion. I wonder if Frog forgot to take his bath last night and I'd gotten used to his stink.

I began to sing my song, but Zion didn't look impressed. She stared toward my house like she couldn't wait to leave. Then, right in the middle of my song, her momma walked outside. Zion stood up and took off. "I gotta go."

I thought about hollering, "How do you think I did? Do I sound like I'm singing from my heart now?" But I changed my mind because of the way she'd treated Frog.

I was so mad, I took it out on him. "Get over here, Frog. Let me get a good whiff of you." Frog obeyed. I took a deep breath through my nose. He smelled as sweet as honeysuckles. Some folks have peculiar ways, and clearly Zion Washington is one of them.

Fuming over rude people
(but not for long),
Tate P.

March 12, 1949

Dear Mr. Williams,

TODAY IS MY BIRTHDAY. I woke up to the sound of the light ping of rain hitting our roof. A moment later sheets of rain came down, and thunder growled in the distance. When a bolt of lightning cracked the sky, Lovie crawled under my bed and whimpered. This is not the way anyone wants to start off her birthday. But folks should never let the weather decide what sort of day they're going to have. So I put on my happy face and wandered into the kitchen.

Silly Uncle Jolly stood in front of the stove, banging an iron skillet with a serving spoon. He started singing some made-up song. He sang it to the tune of "The Farmer in the Dell." "*The birthday girl is up, the birthday girl is up. Ding Dong, jig-a-long, the birthday girl is up. It's pancake day today, it's pancake day today. Ding Dong, jig-a-long, it's pancake day today.* How many pancakes do you want, Sweet Tater?"

Aunt Patty Cake walked in and poured herself a cup of coffee. "I believe I like your birthday almost as much as you do."

I decided to take full advantage of Aunt Patty Cake's good mood. "Can Lovie stay inside until it stops raining?"

"After she does her business. You'll need to dry her off before she steps back in this house."

Lovie did her business real quick. She didn't want to miss any of the fun. Of course the boy who loves yams but hates pancakes decided to sleep in.

Garnett helped celebrate my birthday that night. Aunt Patty Cake made fried chicken, dirty rice, and a chocolate cake. I got a pair of black Mary Janes from her and Uncle Jolly and a new Nancy Drew book from Garnett.

After I opened my gifts, Garnett asked, "Tate, have you planned a dress rehearsal? You could rehearse in front of us."

Mr. Williams, by now you're an expert about dress rehearsals. I'd figured Miss Mildred would want to have one with me too. Last week I told her that I was entering the singing category of the contest. Her mouth hung open a long time. It hung open so long, a fly flew inside and she sputtered and shook her head like it was on fire.

Then she repeated what I'd heard her say when I first wanted to take voice lessons. "You know, Tate, some voices aren't meant to be heard."

This time, I said, "Yes, ma'am, that's a fact. And it's a pity Verbia Calhoon don't know that." Miss Mildred's mouth went back to catching flies again.

I decided to take Garnett's suggestion and use my family as my dress-rehearsal audience. Considering Uncle Jolly and Aunt Patty Cake's reaction to my announcement, I was real nervous. Not to mention Zion's low opinion of my talent. But if I'm not ready now, I'll never be. And this was my birthday. Good things were bound to happen.

I had to sing without music, but I'd been practicing that way. I stood in front of them in the living room. Garnett patted Uncle Jolly's knee, and he squeezed her hand. Aunt Patty Cake examined her fingernails. Frog sat cross-legged on the floor, smiling.

Finally I took a big breath and opened my mouth. I pretended I was in bed next to Momma and we were singing together like old times. I closed my eyes to help take me there. And when I finished the song, I opened them.

Aunt Patty Cake had tears running down her eyes, and Uncle Jolly looked like he could catch a few flies himself.

Garnett pressed her hands together. "Oh my, Tate!"

"I still have some time to practice," I said.

"That was beautiful," Garnett said. "I can't imagine it being any better."

"When did you start sounding like your momma?" Uncle Jolly asked, which is about the best thing anyone ever said to me.

And then Aunt Patty Cake wiped her eyes and announced, "I'm going to make you a new dress."

Which should have been the nicest offer to hear, especially after knowing Aunt Patty Cake hadn't taken to the idea of me singing. Unfortunately Aunt Patty Cake is not the best seamstress in the parish. The last time she tried to make me a dress, she accidentally sewed up the armholes. Thank goodness she got frustrated and gave up. But now she looked determined, and I don't think a dress made by Aunt Patty Cake could hold up to Verbia Calhoon's golden curls.

Happier, but fretting some
about my festival dress,
Tate P.

Dear Mr. Williams,

AUNT PATTY CAKE didn't wait for the temperatures to grow warm. As soon as she heard about the special fabric sale at Bolton High School, she made plans for my competition dress. The ad in the *Town Talk* said there were thousands and thousands of yards of chambray in every color and pattern. I hope Aunt Patty Cake didn't decide to think I'd look darling in polka dots. Thank goodness before she drove away for the sale last night, she rolled down the window and asked, "What's your favorite color?"

"Blue," I said.

"Perfect." Aunt Patty Cake put the car in drive, and I didn't see her until this morning.

The blue fabric is beautiful. It has a purple hint to it, like the lilac chaste tree in Irma Bitters's yard. That morning, I stood there admiring it draped over Aunt Patty

Cake's bed. It's a downright pity, because with Aunt Patty Cake as the seamstress, this is the best that fabric is ever going to be.

Garnett thought it was pretty too. She stroked the fabric. "You are going to look gorgeous at the talent show."

I sure hope Aunt Patty Cake manages to sew on the sleeves this time.

I need to forget about that dress and concentrate on my singing. I'm curious, Mr. Williams, does someone make those cowboy shirts for you?

> Trying to stay focused
> on my song,
> Tate P.

March 25, 1949

Dear Mr. Williams,

WHEN I LEFT FOR SCHOOL Monday morning, Aunt
Patty Cake was laying out the pattern pieces of my dress.
I would have asked to see the cover, but she had a mouth-
ful of pins and she didn't glance up when I walked into
the kitchen. Frog and I ate bread and fig preserves on
the front porch. Aunt Patty Cake didn't bother saying
good-bye when I hollered to tell her I was leaving to
meet the school bus.

That afternoon, when the school bus dropped me
off at home, I left Lovie on the front porch and went
inside. Aunt Patty Cake was sitting in front of her black
Singer.

"Hi, Aunt Patty Cake," I called out.

With her back to me, she lifted her hand in a quick
wave. That afternoon I heard words I'd never heard coming out of her mouth. I can't write them here, but to give

you an idea, Frog and me would have had our mouths washed out with soap if we'd whispered them under our breath. I was getting real nervous thinking about how that blue dress was going to turn out. I guess it would be better to be laughed at because of my dress than because of my singing.

Before I went to bed, I ducked my head inside the kitchen. Aunt Patty Cake was glaring across the room, and I swear there was meanness shooting out of her eyes. When I realized her focus was the blue fabric wadded up in the corner next to the broom, my stomach felt like someone was squeezing it hard. That night, I tossed and turned, and when I finally fell asleep I dreamed of wearing a dress that not only had missing armholes but also no place for my neck to come through either. I was a blue ghost.

The next morning, Aunt Patty Cake wasn't by the sewing machine. She was sitting in her straight chair, listening to you sing as she ripped out a seam. Oh, how I wish Constance Washington was making my dress.

When I came home, I was in for a surprise. The blue dress was hanging on the back of my bedroom door. Miracle of miracles! It wasn't hemmed yet, but it was beautiful! I half suspected someone, maybe Garnett, came over in the middle of the night and finished it. Although I didn't even know if Garnett knew how to sew.

I ran out of the room and hugged Aunt Patty Cake, who'd been dozing in her chair with her feet resting atop a Delightfully Devine Beauty Products box. I told her how the dress was perfect and how she was the best aunt in the entire parish and maybe in the great state of Louisiana.

She hugged me, then held me at arms' length with her hands resting on my shoulders. She sighed and said, "Tate, I hate to break this to you, baby, but I'm never sewing another thing for the rest of my entire life."

I don't understand why a person would give up on something after they finally got the hang of it. I'm never, ever giving up on singing, and neither should you, Mr. Williams.

Singing forever and ever,
Tate P.

Dear Mr. Williams,

LATELY LOVIE HASN'T BEEN meeting me at the mailbox when I get off the school bus. Uncle Jolly says she has wanderlust and that I shouldn't worry about her, because she's always home by dinner. But it makes me think she's not happy here if she goes gallivanting. Uncle Jolly's right, though. She always comes home by dinner, waiting for me to put scraps in the old aluminum pie dish.

Mrs. Applebud was in our kitchen this afternoon, drinking a cup of coffee and eating a slice of pecan pie with Aunt Patty Cake.

"Mrs. Applebud has good news. Her son and his new family will be moving here by next fall."

"I hope you and Keiko can be good friends," Mrs. Applebud said. "She'll need some help with English. Although she's already learning."

"Maybe she can teach me Japanese," I said. It was funny how the Japanese seemed like enemies a few months ago, but Coolie's and Theo Grace's pen pals helped me see Japan differently. I guess that's what Mrs. Kipler meant when she said we'd get to know new worlds. Although I don't think Wallace or his family is going to be excited about Yuki and Keiko moving here. And probably some other families too.

Later that night, Aunt Patty Cake was ironing a basket of laundry while she hummed to the radio.

I asked her, "Where will Albert and his new family live?"

"What do you mean?" Aunt Patty Cake asked.

"Will they have to live in Pine Bend?"

Aunt Patty Cake frowned. "Why in the world would you think that? They'll probably live with Mrs. Applebud. She has plenty of room."

"Well, good. You can call on them personally for your Delightfully Devine products."

She seemed annoyed by my remark. I was just wanting her to win that Dream Dust Derby. She was still frowning as she sprinkled starch over Uncle Jolly's collar. When she finished, that shirt was so stiff, it could have stood up on its own.

Relieved Aunt Patty Cake
skipped the starch on
my clothes,
Tate P.

Dear Mr. Williams,

LAST NIGHT WAS the season opening for the Alexandria
Aces. I'd been rehearsing for the talent show every day,
so I was glad when Uncle Jolly announced we'd be going
to the game. I needed a break. Uncle Jolly's truck was in
the shop, so we took Aunt Patty Cake's car. Frog and
me climbed in back, where Uncle Jolly's baseball glove
lay on the floorboard. "Reckon this will be the big night
you catch a foul ball?"

"You never know," Uncle Jolly said. "Either way,
I'll be ready."

You should have seen Uncle Jolly's face when we
picked up Garnett and she walked out of her little house
with her very own baseball glove.

Our seats were so high up that they should have both
left their gloves at home. But these are two dreamers,
and whenever they heard the crack of the bat they both

held their gloves like the ball was going to fly their way. Anyone could tell Uncle Jolly and Garnett were crazy about each other, but I could see them peering out of the corner of their eyes, sizing up the other's glove. One time, Uncle Jolly caught her scoping his glove out, and he held his stare until her eyes met up with his. When they did, she just smiled and Uncle Jolly melted like he always does when Garnett flashes her pearly whites at him.

Frog and I were getting hungry, and so I asked Uncle Jolly for a cotton candy. Uncle Jolly flagged down the boy carrying a tray of the pink spun sugar. He was digging in his pocket to get out his wallet when John Tidwell stepped up to bat. When we heard the pop of the bat, Uncle Jolly was handing the boy a dollar. The ball flew up over the backstop and soared through the air above us.

Holding up her glove, Garnett jumped to her feet. Uncle Jolly was taking change from the boy when the ball landed with a *smack* in Garnett's mitt. And when Uncle Jolly handed the cotton candy to me, Garnett yelled, "Hot dog!"

Uncle Jolly waved to a hot-dog boy, then he did a double take.

Garnett held the ball under Uncle Jolly's nose. "Look!"

Uncle Jolly's chin dropped. He'd been trying for years to experience what Garnett had accomplished. It happened right next to him, and he hadn't even witnessed it.

But I had, and I said, "Hot dog, Garnett!"

Uncle Jolly sent the hot dog boy away with a "Never mind."

After the game, Garnett rushed out to the field to get her ball signed by all the players. She asked us to come too, but Uncle Jolly shook his head, and Frog and me decided to stay put also. Besides, it was fun to watch Garnett from the bleachers. She was more entertaining than the game. Waving her arms around, probably telling them how she caught the ball. She asked them to sign her glove, too. I could tell they didn't mind none. Garnett is a looker, after all.

I know Uncle Jolly thinks Garnett is the cat's meow, but the way he sat up there waiting for her to finish getting those autographs, you'd have thought she was his number one enemy. Garnett chattered all the way home about what the players said to her. Uncle Jolly tried to act as if he wasn't listening, but he was soaking in every word like biscuits sopping up gravy.

When we arrived at Garnett's house, I was afraid Uncle Jolly was so mad that he'd forget he was a gentleman. But he put the car in park and walked around to open the passenger door. And when he did, Garnett said, "James, close your eyes, and I'll give you a big surprise."

Uncle Jolly must have heard this before, because he leaned toward her, shut his eyes, and puckered his lips. Garnett grabbed his hand and placed the autographed baseball in his palm. Uncle Jolly opened his eyes and looked down. Then she kissed him on the cheek and dashed off.

"Good night, Tate! Better luck next time, James!" she hollered, and giggled all the way to the front door.

Fan of Hank Williams,
the Alexandria Aces, and
Garnett Bilmont,
Tate P.

April 22, 1949

Dear Mr. Williams,

LOVIE DIDN'T COME HOME last night. Aunt Patty Cake said she was making a pan of cornbread when she'd noticed Lovie pass the kitchen window. She figured Lovie was visiting Gayle Rockfire's place, but when Mr. Rockfire dropped by this morning for coffee he said he hadn't seen her in two days.

When I got home from school, I headed toward my bicycle, determined to find Lovie. Frog followed me, and I knew exactly what was on his mind.

"You don't have a bicycle anymore," I reminded him. I thought about letting him ride on my handlebars, but then I looked down at his feet. Frog was wearing Big Pete's boots. Just when I'd thought I'd seen the last of them—he must have dug them out of the trash after Uncle Jolly threw them out.

"Well, if you come with me, you can't wear those boots," I said.

He turned and stomped off.

I was glad Frog wasn't going. He would have slowed me down. I jumped on my bike and took off toward the road.

Aunt Patty Cake hollered for me from the front porch. "If you'll wait a second, we can go in the car."

I told her I wanted to use my bike because I could go places a car couldn't, places a dog might think about hiding. When I said those words, I had a choke in my throat. Why would Lovie want to hide from me? No one here had mistreated her. Even though Aunt Patty Cake scared her something terrible when she yelled at Lovie for wetting my bed, she'd dropped a crispy bacon strip for her on the floor an hour later.

I pushed off and pedaled away from home.

Aunt Patty Cake called, "Be back before dark, Tate!"

Canton Cemetery Road turned into a blur, but I braked every time I thought I saw something move in the grass. I rode down to the Kizers' place and knocked on their door. Ebby answered, and I could tell she was wearing Florida Sunrise Pink on her lips. If I hadn't been on such an important mission, I would have told her how nice she looked. When I asked if she'd seen Lovie, she said, "No, I'm sorry, Tate. I'm afraid I've never seen your dog. Let me ask Newman."

She asked me to step inside, but I said, "No, ma'am, thank you. I'll wait out here."

Then Ebby called out to Newman. I heard the Carter Family singing from the back of the house. Newman walked up behind Ebby and peered at me over his glasses. He had the *Alexandria Town Talk* in his hand.

"Tate is looking for her dog," Ebby said, resting her hand against Newman's chest.

Newman's eyebrows met. "What's your dog look like, Tate? I see dogs all the time walking up and down this road."

"Lovie is a Louisiana cur dog, leopard colored and icy blue eyes." I'd practiced saying that all the way there.

Newman raised his eyebrows. "That's your dog?"

My heart beat like a broken clock. That's what a slice of hope can do to you. "Yes, sir!"

"I saw that dog. Hard to forget those eyes. Yes'm, I

saw her a couple of days ago heading toward Gayle Rockfire's place."

My heart sank. "Yes, sir," I told him, "Lovie visits Mr. Rockfire and Corky a lot, but Mr. Rockfire hasn't seen her today."

Newman scratched his head. "I'm sorry, little gal. Wish I could be a bigger help, but I'll keep my eye out for Lovie from now on."

"Sorry, Tate," Ebby said. "Don't worry too much. I'll bet anything she'll show up. A dog remembers the place that loves her most."

I decided to ride over to Mr. Rockfire's again. Maybe I'd find Lovie along the way. As I pedaled up the hill, I stopped anyplace that I thought Lovie might like. When I noticed an opening in some underbrush beside the road, I stopped my bike. After dropping on all fours, I crawled over to take a peek inside. The only thing I found was a sack of garbage someone had tossed out. Down the road a piece, I saw an abandoned car that had been there a long time, although no one had figured out how it got there. Frog and I used to pretend we were driving that car, until a snake crawled out from under the seat. It was just a harmless brown snake, but it kept us from returning. Nothing could keep me away today. I braced myself and opened the door on the driver's side. I looked in the front and back. I whispered her name aloud— "Lovie, Lovie"—but I didn't see or hear a peep.

The sun was setting low in the sky, so I straddled my bike and headed back on the road. At Mr. Rockfire's house, Corky was lying on the porch. He stood when I approached and barked. He barked so much that I started to wonder what Lovie saw in him. I was relieved he had a chain leash attached to his collar. Thank goodness Mr. Rockfire finally came outside. One of the straps from his overalls was undone. "Is that you, Tate?"

"Yes, sir."

"Still looking for Lovie?"

"Yes, sir." My throat felt thick. I could hardly talk. I was grateful Mr. Rockfire was doing it for me.

"Tate, sorry to say I haven't seen her, but I've got a feeling she'll show up at either your place or mine. If it's mine, I'll get her back home quicker than a sneeze."

I nodded, because that's all I could do.

Mr. Rockfire must have understood exactly what I needed to know, because he said, "Tate, you've been real good to that dog. She'll come home."

I waved before pedaling back to our house. I didn't cover half of Rippling Creek, but I planned to start out again first thing in the morning.

Mr. Williams, you write a lot of heartache songs. Is that because you lost something you really loved?

Hoping your life is going
better than mine,
Tate P.

April 25, 1949

Dear Mr. Williams,

IT'S BEEN THREE DAYS, and Lovie has not returned. I don't want to think about what could happen to a sweet dog out there alone in the world. We missed your show on Saturday because we were busy looking for her. And you know we never miss the *Louisiana Hayride*. Aunt Patty Cake asked, "You reckon Lovie is trying to find her way back to Texas?"

Now, if that wasn't the dumbest idea I ever did hear. Why would a dog that had its bark beaten out of her ever want to go back to her old home?

By now everyone in Rippling Creek knows about her being gone. At school, Mrs. Kipler asked the principal if there was anything they could do. You know your dog is really lost when the principal of Rippling Creek School writes an official announcement and orders every teacher in every class to read it.

When Mrs. Kipler read it to ours, everybody turned to me with the most pitiful looks, including Verbia. And if there is anything I hate, it is someone like Verbia Calhoon feeling sorry for me. All day in school, I drew pictures of Lovie. I drew a doghouse with a soft bed of her own made with pillows and Aunt Patty Cake's wedding quilt (Lovie always liked that quilt). I got so caught up daydreaming that I didn't listen to Theo Grace read her letter from her pen pal. Mrs. Kipler peered down at my drawing when she walked by my desk, but she didn't say anything.

I guess it will come as no surprise to you that I won't be singing at the Rippling Creek May Festival. Can't see the point in it now. When a person's heart is breaking, the idea of getting onstage and singing seems like a lousy idea. I hope you don't take that personal, Mr. Williams. I guess that's how we're different. I can't sing because my heart is breaking, and you sing because yours is.

> Waiting for Lovie with a big
> hole in my heart,
> Tate P.

PS—Mr. Williams, if you do happen to see a leopard-colored Louisiana Catahoula dog with icy-blue eyes around Shreveport, please let me know. She's awful shy, but she knows her name. So all you'd have to do is call out "Lovie" in a sugar voice (the same tone you use when you sing "My Sweet Love Ain't Around"), and I'm sure she'd come to you.

April 27, 1949

Dear Mr. Williams,

THERE IS AN EMPTY CORNER in my room that rips me
to pieces whenever I look at it. I guess you know what
that means. Lovie still hasn't returned. Aunt Patty Cake
wrote Momma about it, and Momma wrote me a letter.
I'll share it with you. It said:

> DEAR TATE,
> You're in my prayers and thoughts right now. We both
> know what it's like to lose someone special to us. And
> now you're having to go through it again with Lovie.
> I can't promise that Lovie will show up. I wish I
> could. I will say this, though. After Jolly told me
> about Lovie, I knew you gave her a better home than
> her last. That should make you feel proud. Lovie must
> have her reasons if she hasn't come back. Please don't
> give up hope, but don't give up getting on with things.

*It's hard to lose our loved ones, but they would want*
*us to go on. You should reconsider singing at the May*
*Festival. It will do you good to focus on something.*

LOVE,
MOMMA

Mr. Williams, I know this sounds terrible, but that letter made me mad (and I'm still mad about it!). How could Momma compare Elroy Broussard and Big Pete leaving to Lovie's gone missing? I told Aunt Patty Cake how I wish she hadn't told Momma and how those two men don't have a thing in the world in common with a true-blue dog like Lovie.

Aunt Patty Cake said, "I don't think that's who your momma meant at all."

Lonesome for Lovie,
Tate P.

April 30, 1949

Dear Mr. Williams,

As HARD AS THIS LETTER will be for me to write, I know it's the best thing to do because I, Tate P. Ellerbee, am a loyal friend. When I tell it all, you might regret the day you ever heard my name.

Today has been a year long. You know how I've been in a slump, moping around because of Lovie taking off? She'd been gone nine days. I'd poured such loving into that dog, I couldn't for the life of me understand why she'd leave. We all looked for her—Uncle Jolly and Garnett drove the roads between here and Lecompte and then went the other direction, toward Glenmora, hoping to meet up with her or anyone who might have noticed a precious dog with icy-blue eyes and a tip of white on her tail.

Aunt Patty Cake seemed to take it almost as hard as me. Maybe she felt guilty because she'd seen Lovie go off, but she'd figured Lovie would come back like the other times. Aunt Patty Cake asked everyone in her territory if they'd seen Lovie. No one had. It's hard to find a dog that doesn't bark. Nobody seems to pay her any mind.

Today I was sitting on the porch licking my wounds about Lovie when I saw Mrs. Applebud come out of her house. If you guessed it was two o'clock in the afternoon, you're right. Mrs. Applebud cut the last of her purple azaleas, gathered them together in a bouquet, and put them in a mason jar. Then she began slowly crossing the street toward the cemetery.

I was so deep into my pity party, I almost didn't hear Rudy's convertible. It was too early for the paper, but I knew the sound of his car. His muffler grew louder. I took off after Mrs. Applebud.

My legs moved so fast they seemed to turn into wings. I felt like I was flying. My head pounded, remembering the times Rudy zoomed by our house. Frog would race after him, leaning over the handlebars, pressing Big Pete's boots against the pedals. I remember Rudy's arm stretched high into a wave as he left Frog behind. Frog could never beat him. But today I would.

Rudy's car appeared around the bend just as I reached Mrs. Applebud. His brakes screeched. I grabbed Mrs. Applebud's arm. She seemed startled, but her tiny feet met my pace as we rushed together to the other side.

I fell first. Mrs. Applebud collapsed on top of me. Rudy jumped out and rushed over to us. He pulled Mrs. Applebud to her feet with a jolt. Some of her hair fell from her tight bun as she wobbled, trying to catch her balance.

"Sorry, Mrs. Applebud. I wasn't paying no mind." Sweat poured down Rudy's pimply face.

I hopped up and pushed against his chest. "You should have been paying a mind!" I shoved him, again. "You could have killed her!"

Rudy nodded nervously and slowly backed away.

"I'm sorry." He looked over his shoulder, staring toward the road.

"Going fast ain't that important," I told him. "Being the fastest doesn't mean a thing!"

Rudy asked Mrs. Applebud, "Can I help you home?"

Mrs. Applebud shook her head and tucked some of her hair behind her ear. "No, son, but slow down. Don't need to rush through life."

"Yes, ma'am." Rudy wiped his face with his sleeve. "I'm awful sorry." He kept muttering "sorry, sorry" as he eased backward toward his car. Then he got inside and started the engine. He took off so slowly, I do believe Mrs. Applebud would have beat his car in a race.

We watched him in silence for what seemed like forever until he left our sight. Aunt Patty Cake's car appeared from around the bend. She was returning from her deliveries. She started down our driveway, then suddenly stopped the car.

Mrs. Applebud fixed her eyes on me. With a small smile, she held out her hand. "It's just a piece away," she said softly.

Directly beyond her was the Canton Cemetery entrance. Headstones dotted the land. I froze, not wanting to step any closer. And that's when I caught a glimpse of brown. It looked like a dog. My dog.

I gasped. Words couldn't reach my tongue.

The dog moved quickly and disappeared into the woods that lined the edge of the cemetery.

My first impulse was to run toward her, but instead I surprised myself and took hold of Mrs. Applebud's hand. I let her guide me through the entrance and toward a grave under a big sycamore tree. Birds flew by, and a squirrel darted in front of us, then climbed onto a low branch. Canton Cemetery was not the scary place I'd imagined. It was peaceful and pretty. I stared at the place where I thought I'd seen Lovie. Now I was only a few yards away from the spot where she'd entered the woods.

Mrs. Applebud inched over and placed the few surviving azaleas atop the grave. Then she picked up a dried bouquet and stepped aside. Her gaze met mine.

I thought about taking off into the woods to see if that dog was definitely Lovie, but something was holding me there. Something so strong, I couldn't explain it for a million years. I just knew deep in my gut if I stepped away, it would have been wrong. My heart felt like it was trying to leave my chest. I didn't want to look, because then I'd know without a doubt it had happened.

Mrs. Applebud was waiting. I took a deep breath and read the words on the gravestone: JAMES IRWIN ELLERBEE (FROG).

*It had happened.*

Remember, Mr. Williams, how I told you I don't cry? Well, I wasn't lying about that. But right there in front of Frog's grave, seeing it for the first time, a lump gathered in my throat. It didn't let loose until I whispered, "Oh, Frog."

For a long moment, a hush seemed to fall over us. Then I heard grass swishing. Someone was moving in our direction. My vision was blurry, but I could make out a tall figure with dark hair—Aunt Patty Cake.

When she reached me, she slipped her arm around my shoulders, offering her apron.

I buried my face in it.

"Let it all out, honey," she said.

And as I began to remember it all, I did just what my aunt Patty Cake told me to do.

Mr. Williams, it happened last June, two months before you arrived in Shreveport and sang on the *Louisiana Hayride*. Momma had been gone for eight long months. Frog and me were riding our bicycles all around Rippling Creek. That day, when people waved at us, we ignored them. We were on a mission. We were going to find us some Reds.

We'd been riding all morning without a sign, and

when we reached the fork I pointed to Sampson Road, telling Frog, "You go that way and I'll go down Fish Hatchery Road. Then let's meet back at headquarters." Headquarters was the code name for our magnolia tree.

Frog took off fast. I watched him because I knew he'd lean back and raise his front wheel like he always did when I gave him an assignment. Then he pedaled like the wind. Those Reds couldn't outrace Frog.

I made my way down Fish Hatchery Road. I was busy scanning right and left, looking for a Red, when I heard the train. I remember thinking everything sure runs like clockwork in Rippling Creek.

Then I remembered the railroad crossing at Sampson Road. No one lived near that crossing, and Sampson Road wasn't traveled much. Frog would be crossing that track just about that time. Frog thought he could out-run everyone and everything, even the Missouri Pacific. I stared down at my watch. One o'clock. I turned my bike around so sharp that I fell off and skinned my knees. I quickly picked the bike up and hopped back on. I pedaled as fast and hard as I could. I could hear the train approaching—*chugga chugga choo, chugga chugga choo.* The whistle blew. When I reached the fork and turned onto Sampson Road, I saw a ribbon of steam rising above the longleaf pines.

The whistle blew and blew. I pedaled and pedaled. And when the train screeched to a slow halt, I slammed my brakes. I fell again, but this time I stayed down because somehow I knew I was too late.

The sheriff said the best he could gather was Frog had gotten his bicycle wheel jammed between the railroad cross-ties. He was probably trying to get it loose when the train approached. The sheriff said, "It was over before Frog knew what happened."

But I figured out another part that no one had to tell me. You see, Mr. Williams, Big Pete's boots were to the side of the tracks. I knew how Frog loved those boots. He must have slipped them off and thrown them to the side before he tried to get the bicycle free from the track. I guess Frog thought he was saving our daddy by saving those boots.

Now you know it all, Mr. Williams. You probably believe I'm a bold-faced liar who has led you down a road of deception with my stories about Frog. But until today in Canton Cemetery, Frog was never dead to me. I didn't go to the funeral. No matter how much Aunt

Patty Cake tried to shame me into it, saying, "Your momma can't go, and she'd want you to," I wouldn't listen. And when I heard the screen door slam shut as she and Uncle Jolly left the house for the service, I saw Frog in the corner of my room. We had a good laugh about everyone thinking he was dead.

So when I told you those stories about Frog listening to me sing and pestering me, I really did believe he was here. I guess because I wanted so badly for him to be.

Here's the strangest thing about the longest day ever. Me who never cries was out there in the cemetery, breaking down. I sobbed so loud, it felt like the ground trembled. Just as I was blowing my nose into Aunt Patty Cake's apron I felt something licking the back of my knee. I looked down. Lovie was working on a scrape that I wasn't aware I had until that moment. I guess it happened when I fell with Mrs. Applebud.

But just as I went to pet my dog, Lovie took off toward the woods. I wanted to holler, "Don't leave me now when I need you most."

"I think Lovie wants to show us something," Aunt Patty Cake said. "Maybe she finally caught a squirrel."

The three of us left Frog's grave site and headed to

the spot where Lovie entered the woods. We didn't have to go far. She was just a few feet away, stretched out so all her babies could nurse, all three of them gray and plump.

"Puppies!" I restrained myself from grabbing up one. They didn't look anything like Lovie. But they were the spitting image of Mr. Rockfire's dog, Corky.

Aunt Patty Cake grinned. "Well, my word! It never occurred to me."

"She didn't seem big enough," said Mrs. Applebud.

The way Lovie licked one of her younguns, I could tell she was a good momma. "Maybe Uncle Jolly will have a squirrel dog after all."

"One of them is bound to be like their daddy," Aunt Patty Cake said.

Looking at those puppies nurse Lovie made me realize she hadn't run away from me. She was just trying to make sure her babies would be safe. In a way, finding Lovie helped me to finally find the truth about Frog.

At home, Aunt Patty Cake tucked her wedding quilt inside an empty Delightfully Devine Beauty Products box, and we moved Lovie and her babies to the back porch. As hard as it was, I kept my distance from them. I didn't want Lovie to run away again.

Mr. Williams, how do I explain a day like today? A day filled with lots of sad and happy, too.

Tonight I asked Aunt Patty Cake that very question. She said, "Baby, that's called life."

Hoping you'll understand,
Tate P.

Dear Mr. Williams,

THE MORNING AFTER I saw Frog's grave for the first time, I lay in bed, studying the ceiling, feeling like I could float up to it. Everything that had felt jumbled in my head now seemed so clear. I knew I had to write the judge about Momma. I wanted to write that letter. A moment later I was sitting on the edge of my bed with a pen and tablet. I told the judge Miss Jordie June Ellerbee was my momma and I needed her something fierce at home. I explained how I was proud that Momma had been a Goree Girl but that she had a bigger plan to share her gift with the world. She was missing out on important things like me singing at the Rippling Creek May Festival Talent Contest and I could have used some pointers.

The last part of the letter was the hardest because it was about Frog. I spilled my true feelings all over that page. I told him how I'd been so upset that Momma wasn't here last summer when Frog had his accident. I'd needed her then more than any time in my life, and when she didn't show up I didn't answer any of her letters or postcards. What happened to Frog wasn't Momma's fault or mine. I know that now, but we needed to see each other through that hard time. And in closing I told the judge I didn't see how a person making one mistake like driving a car for someone like Elroy Broussard should be kept from being a momma to me.

By the time Mrs. Applebud's rooster crowed, I knew I was going to sing in the talent show. And never mind that I'd been practicing "Wildwood Flower" for months. I was going to sing Frog's favorite song, "You Are My Sunshine." This was the right song. I knew it all the way down to my toes.

At breakfast I announced my decision to Aunt Patty Cake. She was so happy I'd changed my mind about dropping out of the talent show that she said, "Come on. Let's go to the Kizers' and make a telephone call." The Kizers had the only phone within a mile from us. Sure enough, Mr. Kizer was doing his crossword puzzle, and Mrs. Kizer was listening to *Queen for a Day*. But they seemed more interested in what Aunt Patty Cake was saying to Miss Mildred. "Tate has decided to sing 'You Are My Sunshine,' so please bring that sheet music instead."

I don't know what Miss Mildred said, but it sure made Aunt Patty Cake mad, because she told her, "Mildred Dupree, I don't care what you think about Tate's new song, I expect you to play it. Unless you don't know how to play that song. If you don't, then I'll arrange for another accompanist." And then Aunt Patty Cake said something I never thought I'd hear her admit. "My niece, Jordie June, the lead singer of the Goree Girls, has a lot of connections. I'm sure she knows every talented pianist in the parish." Well, that's all Aunt Patty Cake had to say.

The next day, at the talent show, wouldn't you know, Verbia Calhoon went first. Mrs. Calhoon probably arranged it so that the judges would forget how bad Verbia's singing was and only remember her golden curls. I was glad I wasn't first, but I sure didn't want to be last, which was exactly when I was scheduled. Though I did get to move up a spot because Lenny Robbins locked his knees during his harmonica performance and fainted a minute into his song.

When I walked onto the stage, I stood behind the microphone, gazed out, and spotted Mrs. Applebud. She'd dozed through Verbia's song but now was wide awake. From her bench she gave me a small nod. Aunt Patty Cake sat to her right, straight as an ironing board. Next to her, Uncle Jolly and Garnett held hands, watching me. Then those lovesick hounds turned to each other at that exact moment and smiled. Seeing my family in the audience, I knew I'd make it through the song. And even though Frog wasn't sitting out there, I felt like he was near me.

Funny, I don't remember hearing the words when I sang. Does that ever happen to you? All that was going through my head were the good times—Momma and me singing in bed, Uncle Jolly taking me to the circus, modeling for Aunt Patty Cake, getting Lovie, and riding bicycles with Frog. I reckon you could say the best of my life was wrapped up in that song. Now, standing on that stage, I knew exactly what Zion meant about singing from the heart.

I'm almost forgetting to tell you—I won first place in the singing category! And that wasn't the best part of the day.

*Your fan and First-Place Winner of the Rippling Creek May Festival Talent Contest,*
*Tate P.*

PS—The best part of the day was when they called my name as the first-place winner and Verbia Calhoon got all confused. She stood like they called her name. Why, she beat me to the stage! You should have seen her face when she realized it was Tate P. Ellerbee's name they announced.

PPS—The second-best part was Mrs. Calhoon's face when she learned it too.

PPPS—And Miss Mildred's.

May 15, 1949

Dear Mr. Williams,

AUNT PATTY CAKE continues to surprise me. Yesterday she told me to get into the car, as we needed to make one more delivery.

"Whose delivery?" I asked.

"We're going to see Constance."

Without saying a word, I hightailed it to the car.

We drove up the road and crossed the bridge that stretches over No-Name Creek. Then the gravel road turned into a dirt one that winded through the woods until it met up with a cleared piece of land with about a dozen wood-frame houses. A couple of little girls were drawing in the dirt with a stick, and a few people sat on their porches. Aunt Patty Cake drove up to a white house with blue curtains hanging in the windows.

Constance and Zion came outside to meet us. "I've

been looking forward to that bottle of jasmine bubble bath," Constance said.

Aunt Patty Cake laughed, but I knew she was a little uneasy. She'd looked around after stepping out of the car.

Constance motioned her into the house, and I stayed outside with Zion.

I felt nervous myself, not because we were in Pine Bend, but because I needed to set Zion straight about Frog. I wasn't sure how to do it. I stalled some, telling her about Lovie's puppies and winning first place in the contest. Then I took a big breath and blurted, "Frog is in heaven."

Zion said, "I know."

That nearly knocked me over. "You know?"

"Mm-hm. Momma and me went to his funeral. I thought you be pretending he be here, like an angel. But my momma didn't like me pretending."

I guess that's why Constance popped Zion on the behind that day. I was about to ask her why she never let me know, but Zion has a short attention span.

"You think you could give me one of them puppies?"

Some folks like to get on with things and not harp on the past. Clearly Zion Washington is one of them. She'll have to get behind Uncle Jolly for a puppy. He's trying to size up which one will be a good hunting buddy. He dangles a squirrel tail in front of them and waits to see which puppy takes notice. So far none of them have paid it any mind.

On the drive home, I asked Aunt Patty Cake if we'd be going back to Pine Bend.

"Not to take any orders," she said. "Constance told me she needed a job, and I told her she should think about being a representative for Delightfully Devine Beauty Products. Her neighbors could be her customers."

"But you'd be giving up some of your territory."

Aunt Patty Cake rolled down her window. "I'll be fine," she said.

A breeze blew through the car. Tiny hairs around Aunt Patty Cake's forehead waved, softening her face. Her cheeks had a tinge of pink that wasn't from Forever Rose rouge. She rested her elbow in the open window and started to hum. For the first time, I could imagine that young girl dancing with that Ville Platte boy in the rain. I could picture it as clear as I could see the longleaf pines brush the setting sun as we made our way back home.

There were two packages waiting for us at the house. They were too big to put inside the mailbox, so they'd been left on the screened porch. One was for Aunt Patty Cake and the other was for me!

"Let's pretend it's Christmas and take turns opening them," I said.

Aunt Patty Cake went first. While she tore the package open, I studied the outside of mine. It had all kinds of blue-and-red stamps that looked familiar. Then I realized why. They looked like the stamps Theo Grace and Coolie got on their pen pals' envelopes. This package was from Japan!

Inside Aunt Patty Cake's box were dozens of Delightfully Devine products. She looked confused. "I didn't order these." Then she opened the envelope and read. Her mouth twitched. "Oh well." She tucked the letter back into the envelope. "Didn't win the contest, but I got second prize."

I told her I was sorry. Then I dug through her second-place prize. There was every Delightfully Devine product. I held up one of the boxes. "Aunt Patty Cake, have you ever thought of using Magical Mascara? I'll bet a few coats would bring out your blue eyes."

She laughed and tapped on my package. "Your turn."

When I opened mine, I discovered a card from Keiko saying how she hoped we could be good friends when she moved to Louisiana soon. There was also a present wrapped in floral paper. It was beautiful, I hated to rip it. So I took my time unwrapping it, carefully lifting the tape.

I was so slow, Aunt Patty Cake said, "Hurry, hurry." She'd already forgotten about not winning that contest.

When I got past all the tissue paper, I saw it.

"What the heck is that?" Aunt Patty Cake asked.

"It's a carp streamer," I said, holding it up. How could someone who didn't know me at all send me the most perfect gift?

I explained to Aunt Patty Cake, "It represents a Japanese story about a carp that was so strong, he swam upstream and became a dragon." I might not be a dragon, but ever since Momma left and Frog died, I'd felt like

I'd been trying to swim upstream. And like that carp in the story, I'd made it to the other side.

Seeing the world unfold
before my very eyes,
Tate P.

Dear Mr. Williams,

CONGRATULATIONS ON YOUR new baby boy! I'll bet you'll be a great daddy. He might grow up and be a singer like you.

I wanted you to know how much I enjoyed your farewell performance on the *Louisiana Hayride*. And guess what? I didn't hear it on the radio. I was *there* at the Shreveport Municipal Auditorium. I was the girl sitting smack in the middle of the fifth row. I'm pretty sure you saw me, because you looked my way a lot. I kept wondering, You reckon Mr. Hank Williams knows it's me? But how could you? You don't even know what I look like except that I have plain brown hair and brown eyes and kind of look like my momma (whom you've never seen). So this time I'm sending you a picture of me. That way your curiosity about that girl sitting smack in the middle of the fifth row will be solved. By the way, Aunt Patty Cake says you're prettier in person.

Two days before the show, Uncle Jolly surprised us with tickets. Garnett said she'd never been north of Natchitoches, so she thought the drive alone was an adventure. Garnett is looking different these days, or at least her left hand is. That's right. Uncle Jolly found him a woman that sticks. Aunt Patty Cake forgot about her decision to never sew again and offered to make the wedding dress. Garnett said her yellow suit would do just fine.

You'll be proud to know that I'm taking voice lessons, but I'm not taking them from Miss Mildred. No sirree. Momma wrote that Lulu would be the perfect choice. And Aunt Patty Cake agreed as long as Lulu made a pact not to groom me for the honky-tonk joints (although she didn't say anything about not learning honky-tonk songs).

The best news of all is the judge split Momma's sentence in half. Momma will be home in less than a year. It will be a hard wait, but time is flying and she'll be here before I know it. Aunt Patty Cake says she thinks my letter made a big difference. Until Momma is here, I read her postcards. I've taped every single one on my bedroom walls. Just looking at them makes me feel like she's giving me a great big hug.

Mr. Williams, you're very famous now. The great state of Louisiana will miss you, and so will I. I'll listen to you on the *Grand Ole Opry* and write you when I can. But I hope you won't be disappointed if you don't hear from me as often. My life is busy these days—voice lessons, my cosmetics-modeling job, writing to Keiko, and taking care of Lovie.

Lovie still hasn't barked, but her puppies make up for that. They are yappers! Uncle Jolly picked the noisiest one for his future squirrel dog.

Sometimes Aunt Patty Cake, Lovie, and me go on Mrs. Applebud's cemetery walks. We pay our respects to Mr. Applebud and Frog. On those days, we take them fresh flowers. Aunt Patty Cake says she's not the crying type, but I've seen her pull a handkerchief out of her dress pocket and dab at her eyes. "Those longleaf pines make my eyes water," she claims, but I know she's missing Frog. I know because my eyes water on those cemetery walks too, and it has nothing to do with pine-tree sap.

I try not to dwell on it, but sometimes I think about the things Frog is missing. He'll never know Garnett, play hide-and-seek with Zion, or learn Japanese from Keiko. And he would have loved Lovie as much as I do. I know he would.

Aunt Patty Cake says, "Our loved ones are always with us even after they pass on."

I think that's true, because Canton Cemetery is not where I feel the closest to Frog. I feel his spirit whenever I'm in the places we shared together. I don't see him, but I know he's there.

When I'm riding my bicycle, Lovie likes to follow me. Sometimes I pedal hard and fast like Frog loved to do. I remember him wearing those boots because he thought it made him feel closer to our daddy and how he liked my singing even when it wasn't coming from my heart. And when the wind beats against my face, swear to sweet Sally, I can hear my little brother whispering in my ear, "Whatcha, whatcha?"

So long for now.

Your #1 fan forever,
Tate P. Ellerbee

## Author's Note

Research plays an important part in my writing. Not only does it help me to get the facts straight, it also serves as inspiration for some of the storylines. The process is not unlike a spider spinning her web: Each thread offers a dimension to the story. The following are some of the threads that created Tate's web and became the book *Dear Hank Williams*.

**World War II and the Red Scare.** When I was researching for Tate's story, I needed to understand what it was like to live in postwar America. World War II was the deadliest war in history. More than fifty million people died, many of them civilians.

The war began in 1939, brought on by Adolf Hitler's Poland invasion. It ended in 1945 with the defeat of Nazi Germany and Japan. Even though *Dear Hank Williams* begins three years later, Tate's young life would have been touched by this war since she was two when it started and eight years old when it ended.

Fear and prejudices ran rampant after the war. When I read the *Alexandria Town Talk* from the late 1940s, I came across a lot of articles about the "Reds." Communists were referred to as Reds because of their loyalty to the red Soviet flag. During this time period, people were afraid of what they thought Communists might do. It became known as the Red Scare. When Tate and Frog pretended to be "looking for some Reds," it was a result of this fear.

**Wartime and Postwar Pen Pals.** The pen pal element in the story was inspired by my aunt Barbara's mention of her third-grade teacher arranging for her students to write to Japanese students after the war. Through research, I discovered that during World War II and afterward, some innovative educators around America connected their students with young people living in war-torn countries. One Iowa teacher collected names and addresses of students while on a trip to Europe in the summer of 1939; two of the names were Margot and her sister, Anne Frank. Two Iowa sisters wrote the Franks. They received one reply before the war began and the Franks went into hiding. Since the *Diary of Anne Frank* was one of my favorite books, I was fascinated by this discovery. With that exception of this pen pal experience, I couldn't validate how other educators found the international students. However, I found articles about the rich relationships that formed because of them.

Some relationships lasted decades, sometimes resulting in eventual face-to-face meetings. These pen pal relationships seemed to bridge gaps and heal cultural differences. I hope Tate's classmates' letters from Japan and Tate's eventual choice to write Keiko show this impact.

**Radio Days.** When I was a young child, living in France, my family didn't have a television. We listened to American shows on the military radio broadcasts. This was in the mid-1960s when most families owned a television. I'm grateful for that experience because now I know what it was like for families between the 1930s and 1950s when radio was the main source of entertainment in American households. Tate's family, like most families around the country, could be found in the evenings listening to popular shows such as the *Louisiana Hayride* and the *Grand Ole Opry*. The radio also broadcast the local and national news, including the president's addresses to the country.

***Louisiana Hayride.*** When I was a girl I heard my parents and grandparents mention listening to the *Louisiana Hayride*. It was a radio show that showcased country music. Because of my family's Louisiana roots I always wanted to do a story that included the *Louisiana Hayride*. The venue had a live audience and was broadcast by KWKH from the Shreveport Municipal Auditorium. The first show was broadcast April 3, 1948. Many famous musicians and singers, including Hank Williams, Elvis Presley, and Jerry Lee Lewis, performed there.

**Hank Williams.** When I found out that Hank Williams was a regular performer at the *Louisiana Hayride* during the same time period I planned to write about, I decided to make him part of Tate's story. Although they never meet, I needed to know about his career, especially the time he spent in Louisiana.

Hank Williams was born on September 17, 1923, in Mount Olive, Alabama. He arrived in Shreveport in August 1948, barely known. During his time there, he was a regular on the *Louisiana Hayride*. In December he recorded "Lovesick Blues"; it was released in February 1949 and by March the hit song had rocketed Hank Williams to fame. A few months later his dream had come true—he was invited to be a regular on the *Grand Ole Opry* in Nashville. The *Grand Ole Opry* was similar to the *Louisiana Hayride* but with a larger broadcast area.

**The Goree All Girl String Band.** Years before I created Tate's story, I read a *Texas Monthly* article by Skip Hollandsworth called "O Sister, Where Art Thou?" It was about the Goree All Girl String Band. I never forgot Hollandsworth's article. It was the first seed of inspiration for Tate's story.

Goree State Farm was a prison for women in Huntsville, Texas. In 1940, a group of women prisoners from Goree formed a band. Their first performance was on a Fort Worth radio station, WBAP's *Thirty Minutes Behind the Walls*, a show broadcast from the men's prison in Huntsville and heard across the country. The Goree Girls, their popular name, gathered quite a following, receiving fan mail from all around the broadcast area. The Goree Girls were still enjoying a great popularity during the late 1940s when Tate's story takes place.

# Acknowledgments

Places have always served as powerful touchstones for my work. When I thought I'd lost the love for writing, a place proved that I was wrong. My grandfather had recently moved out of his home and into the Louisiana War Veterans Home when I asked if I could stay at his house and write. He graciously nodded and said, "Yes." I'm thankful to him for that because the first day there I was reminded of the good fortune I have to be born into a family of storytellers. I owed it to them to write my stories.

Two important seeds sprouted this story: Skip Hollandsworth's fine *Texas Monthly* article "O Sister, Where Art Thou?" about a women's prison singing group and a visit to Butters Cemetery. From my grandparents' graves I looked across the road at Pat Tarpley's house and thought, *I wonder what it's like to live across from a small town cemetery.*

My aunt Barbara Larisey shared two important details that contributed to *Dear Hank Williams:* the Camp Claiborne soldiers who marched in front of her home during World War II and the teacher who arranged for her class to have Japanese pen pals after the war ended.

Dr. Miki Crawford, author of *Japanese War Brides in America: An Oral History,* answered my questions, and her book gave me a close-up view of what it must be like to have to acclimate to a postwar culture.

My mother, Brenda Willis, and my daughter, Shannon Holt, listened to my first draft via phone. I appreciate their early encouragement for

Tate's journey. I'm grateful for my dad, Ray Willis, who helped me with technical details in a pivotal scene.

Lois "Sug" Grant enthusiastically read a late draft and made suggestions. Since she is an expert on the charms of central Louisiana, I welcomed and took them.

Over the years, many early drafts of various stories have been read by Charlotte Goebel, Jennifer Archer, Kathi Appelt, Jeanette Ingold, Rebecca Kai Dotlich, and Lola Schaefer. I appreciate and admire these women. Thank you for always telling me the truth.

Amy Berkower liked this story from the first draft she read, and when a writer learns her agent likes her work, she skips around the house in a daze for a while. I'm forever grateful for her support.

I've been publishing for seventeen years with Henry Holt and Company. Each of my books has had the keen attention of managing editor George Wen. He's left the Holt nest now, but I will always appreciate his loving care of my work.

When I visit schools I explain to students that an editor is a teacher. I've been a lucky student because Christy Ottaviano has been my teacher for almost twenty years. She has the sixth sense to know a writer's potential and the talent to help her reach it. Thank you, C.O.

And as always, I'm thankful for Jerry, who twenty years ago, said, "Write."

# Dear Hank Williams

## BONUS MATERIALS

# GOFISH

## QUESTIONS FOR THE AUTHOR

**KIMBERLY WILLIS HOLT**

**What did you want to be when you grew up?**
A writer.

**When did you realize you wanted to be a writer?**
In seventh grade, three teachers encouraged my writing. That was when I first thought the dream could come true. Before that, I didn't think I could be a writer because I wasn't a great student and I read slowly.

**What's your first childhood memory?**
Buying an orange Dreamsicle from the ice-cream man. I was two years old.

**What's your most embarrassing childhood memory?**
In fourth grade, I tried to impress the popular girls that I wanted to be friends with by doing somersaults in front of

them. (I never learned to do cartwheels.) They called me a showoff, so I guess it didn't work. If only I'd known how to do a cartwheel.

**What was your worst subject in school?**
Algebra.

**What was your first job?**
I was in the movies. I popped popcorn at the Westside Cinemas.

**Did you have a special pen pal growing up?**
My great-grandmother was my first pen pal. She wrote to me when my family was living on Guam, and I wrote her back. Then more letters followed.

**What first sparked your interest in writing *Dear Hank Williams*?**
When I read an article in the *Texas Monthly* magazine about the Goree Girls. The title was "O Sister, Where Art Thou?" I knew then that Tate's mom would be a Goree Girl.

**Tate is a very tenacious, forgiving, and inspiring character. What do you find most interesting about her?**
Tate never lets anything keep her down. She is courageous and optimistic.

**Dear Hank Williams is not the only historical coming-of-age novel you've written that takes place in Louisiana. How does this setting inspire you to develop your characters?**

Both sides of my family are from the Central Louisiana area and have been for many generations. My grandparents and parents grew up in Forest Hill, Louisiana. Growing up, I was fascinated by this tiny town and the people there. My parents often talked about their childhoods in a way that made time real to me. I cherish that. Their stories fueled my writing and shaped my character.

**Did this book require a lot of research? How do you usually conduct research for your historical novels?**

All my books take a lot of research. It's important to know the significant events from the time and place that you're writing about. For *Dear Hank Williams*, I read the local newspaper from that period on microfilm. I read the articles, but even the ads contributed to the story. Several Hank Williams biographies helped me build a timeline for the months he was on the *Louisiana Hayride*, the same time that Tate would have been writing him. A book about Japanese war brides gave me insight for an important plot point. I also contacted the author of that book to confirm a detail for my story. Weather matters, too. If a hurricane happened during the time you're writing about, you can't ignore that. For my other books, I've read journals and letters. Each book requires a different journey, and that includes the type of research I do.

**How did you celebrate publishing your first book?**
I'm sure my family went out to dinner. We always celebrate by eating.

**Where do you write your books?**
I write in several places—a soft, big chair in my bedroom, at a table on my screen porch, or at coffee shops.

**Where do you find inspiration for your writing?**
Most of the inspiration for my writing comes from moments in my childhood.

**Which of your characters is most like you?**
I'm a bit like most of them. However, I fashioned Tori in the Piper Reed books after me. But Tori is bossier than I was, and she certainly makes better grades than I did.

**When you finish a book, who reads it first?**
My daughter listens to me read my first draft.

**Are you a morning person or a night owl?**
I'm a morning person.

**What's your idea of the best meal ever?**
That's a toss-up. My grandmother's chicken and dumplings, and sushi.

**Which do you like better: cats or dogs?**
I'm a dog person. I have a poodle named Bronte who is the model for Bruna in the Piper Reed series.

**What do you value most in your friends?**
Loyalty and honesty.

**Where do you go for peace and quiet?**
Home.

**Who is your favorite fictional character?**
Leroy in *Mister and Me* because he is forgiving. And that's a trait many of us don't have.

**What are you most afraid of?**
Anything harming my daughter.

**What time of the year do you like best?**
Fall.

**What is your favorite TV show?**
*CBS Sunday Morning.*

**If you were stranded on a desert island, who would you want for company?**
My husband and daughter.

**What's the best advice you have ever received about writing?**
A writer once told me, "Readers either see what they read or hear what they read. Writers have to learn to write for both." When I started following that advice, my writing improved.

**What do you want readers to remember about your books?**
The characters. I want them to seem like real people. I want them to miss them and wonder what happened to them.

**What would you do if you ever stopped writing?**
I plan on dying with a pen in my hand.

**What do you like best about yourself?**
I'm honest.

**What is your worst habit?**
I eat too much.

**What do you consider to be your greatest accomplishment?**
I gave birth to a wonderful human being.

**What do you wish you could do better?**
I wish I could do a cartwheel.

**What would your readers be most surprised to learn about you?**
I send gift cards with positive messages to myself when I order something for me.

# DISCUSSION QUESTIONS

*Dear Hank Williams* begins in September, when the school year starts, and concludes in June. The discussion questions are based on the months of the school year and the characters and events that are introduced during that time frame.

1.  (September) Describe Tate Ellerbee's home life. What do you know about her mother, father, brother, aunt, and uncle? What other characters impact Tate's life and in what way?

2.  (September) What connections has Tate made to Hank Williams?

3.  (September) Tate always signs her letters in a unique way. Why does she do this and how does it add to the story?

4.  (October) Do you think Hank Williams is reading Tate's letters? Why would he send a second autographed photograph of himself?

5.  (November) Tate explains that she's "not like most folks" (p. 72). What evidence has been given so far that she isn't like the other characters in what she says and what she does?

6.  (November) Why do you think Tate lied about her father being a photographer?

7.  (November) Was there foreshadowing that might have given clues that Tate's mother wasn't an actress? Did Tate lie about her mother or tell half truths about her as a singer?

8.  (November) Tate has revealed a lot about her life. What difficulties has she faced? What is her attitude about her life? What is your opinion about Tate at this point in the book?

9. (December) Why does Wallace "mouth off" whenever the letters and gifts from the Japanese pen pals are shared?

10. (December) Aunt Patty Cake wants Tate to write a letter so the judge might release her mother from prison sooner, but Tate refuses to do so. What are the reasons she gives? Could there be other reasons as well?

11. (December) What do you know about a Louisiana Catahoula cur dog? Why do you think Tate named her dog "Lovie"?

12. (January) Tate writes that "a dog pours a pitcher of love into the lonesome spots of your life. Not that I have many of those. I'm a busy person" (p. 141). Do you think Tate really feels this way? Does keeping busy make a person less lonely?

13. (February) Do you think Tate should sing in the Rippling Creek May Festival Talent Contest? Why or why not?

14. (March) When Zion returns to Tate's house with her mother, she is acting scared. Why do you think she is feeling that way? Does it have anything to do with the previous visit and what happened then?

15. (March) Why does Aunt Patty Cake tell Tate that she is "never sewing another thing for the rest of [her] entire life" after she makes Tate such a beautiful dress (p. 170)?

16. (April) Who do you think Momma is referring to in her letter to Tate when she talks about losing someone they have loved?

17. (April) How did you feel when you learned about Frog? Do you think Tate lied about him?

18. (April) Discuss the events that happened on April 30, 1949. What did Tate learn about herself and about life?

19. (May) There are many symbolic events that occur, such as Aunt Patty Cake driving to Constance Washington's house in Pine Bend and Tate receiving the carp streamer from Keiko. Why are these events important in the story and to the characters?

20. (June) Predict ten years into the future when Tate is an adult. What do you think she will be doing? What will the other members of her family be doing?

**Toby Wilson** is having the toughest summer of his life, with his mother leaving for good and his best friend's brother serving in Vietnam. It's also the summer that Zachary Beaver, the fattest boy in the world, arrives in Toby's sleepy Texas town. Nothing will be the same again.

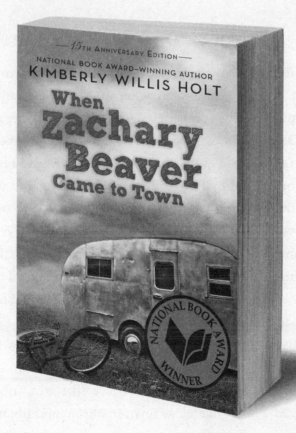

Keep reading for an excerpt.

# Chapter One

Nothing ever happens in Antler, Texas. Nothing much at all. Until this afternoon, when an old blue Thunderbird pulls a trailer decorated with Christmas lights into the Dairy Maid parking lot. The red words painted on the trailer cause quite a buzz around town, and before an hour is up, half of Antler is standing in line with two dollars clutched in hand to see the fattest boy in the world.

Since it's too late in the summer for firecrackers and too early for the Ladybug Waltz, Cal and I join Miss Myrtie Mae and the First Baptist Quilting Bee at the back of the line.

Miss Myrtie Mae wears a wide-brimmed straw hat. She claims that she's never exposed her skin to sun. Even so, wrinkles fold into her face like an unironed shirt. She takes her job as town historian and librarian seriously, and as usual, her camera hangs around her neck. "Toby, how's your mom?"

"Fine," I say.

"That will really be something if she wins."

"Yes, ma'am, it will." My mouth says the words, but my mind is not wanting to settle on a picture of her winning. Mom dreams of following in the footsteps of her favorite singer, Tammy Wynette. Last month she entered a singing contest in Amarillo and won first place. She got a trophy and an all-expense-paid trip to Nashville for a week to enter the National Amateurs' Country Music Competition at the Grand Ole Opry. The winner gets to cut a record album.

Cars and pickups pull into the Dairy Maid parking lot. Some people make no bones about it. They just get in line to see him. Others try to act like they don't know anything about the buzz. They enter the Dairy Maid, place their orders, and exit with Coke floats, chocolate-dipped cones, or curlicue fries, then wander to the back of the line. They don't fool me.

The line isn't moving because the big event hasn't started. Some skinny guy wearing a tuxedo, smoking a pipe, is taking the money and giving out green tickets. Cal could stand in line forever to relieve his curiosity. He knows more gossip than any old biddy in Antler because he gathers it down at the cotton gin, where his dad and the other farmers drink coffee.

"I got better things to do than this," I tell Cal. Like eat. My stomach's been growling all the time now because I haven't had a decent meal since Mom left a few days ago. Not that she cooked much lately since she was getting ready for that stupid contest. But I miss the fried catfish and barbecue dinners she brought home from the Bowl-a-Rama Cafe, where she works.

"Oh, come on, Toby," Cal begs. "He'll probably move out tomorrow and we'll never get another chance."

"He's just some fat kid. Heck, Malcolm Clifton probably has him beat hands down." Malcolm's mom claims he's big boned, not fat, but we've seen him pack away six jumbo burgers. I sigh real big like my dad does when he looks at my report card filled with Cs. "Okay," I say. "But I'm only waiting ten more minutes. After that, I'm splitting."

Cal grins that stupid grin with his black tooth showing. He likes to brag that he got his black tooth playing football, but I know the real story. His sister, Kate, socked him good when he scratched up her Carole King album. Cal says he was sick of hearing "You Make Me Feel Like a Natural Woman" every stinking day of his life.

Scarlett Stalling walks toward the line, holding her bratty sister Tara's hand. Scarlett looks cool wearing a bikini top underneath an open white blouse and hip huggers that hit right below her belly button. With her golden tan and long, silky blond hair, she could do a commercial for Coppertone.

Scarlett doesn't go to the back of the line. She walks over to me. *To me.* Smiling, flashing that Ultra Brite sex appeal smile and the tiny gap between her two front teeth. Cal grins, giving her the tooth, but I lower my eyelids half-mast and jerk my head back a little as if to say, "Hey."

Then she speaks. "Hey, Toby, would ya'll do me a favor?"

"Sure," I squeak, killing my cool act in one split second.

Scarlett flutters her eyelashes, and I suck in my breath. "Take Tara in for me." She passes her little sister's sticky hand like she's handing over a dog's leash. Then she squeezes her fingers into her pocket and pulls out two crumpled dollar bills. I would give anything to be one of those lucky dollar bills tucked into her pocket.

She flips back her blond mane. "I've got to get back home and get ready. Juan's dropping by soon."

The skin on my chest prickles. Mom is right. Scarlett Stalling is a flirt. Mom always told me, "You better stay a spittin' distance from that girl. Her mother had a bad reputation when I went to school, and the apple doesn't fall far from the tree."

Cal punches my shoulder. "Great going, ladies' man!"

I watch Scarlett's tight jeans sway toward her house so she can get ready for the only Mexican guy in Antler Junior High. Juan already shaves. He's a head taller than the rest of the guys (two heads taller than me). That gives him an instant ticket to play first string on our basketball team, even though he's slow footed and a lousy shot. Whenever I see him around town, a number-five-iron golf club swings at his side. I don't plan to ever give him a reason to use it.

"Fatty, fatty, two by four," Tara chimes as she stares at the trailer. "Can't get through the kitchen door."

"Shut up, squirt," I mutter.

Miss Myrtie Mae frowns at me.

Tara yanks on my arm. "Uummmm!" she hollers. "You said shut up. Scarlett!" She rises on her toes as if that makes her louder. "Toby said shut up to me!"

But it's too late. Scarlett has already disappeared across the street. She's probably home smearing gloss on those pouty lips while I hold her whiny sister's lollipop fingers, standing next to my black-toothed best friend, waiting to see the fattest boy in the world.

# Join in the fun and read all the
# Piper Reed Books
## by Kimberly Willis Holt and
## illustrated by Christine Davenier

**Book 1: PIPER REED, NAVY BRAT**

978-0-312-62548-1

**Book 2: PIPER REED, CLUBHOUSE QUEEN**

978-0-312-61676-2

**Book 3: PIPER REED, PARTY PLANNER**

978-0-312-61677-9

**Book 4: PIPER REED, CAMPFIRE GIRL**

978-0-312-67482-3

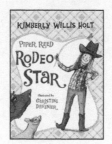

**Book 5: PIPER REED, RODEO STAR**

978-1-250-00409-3

**Book 6: PIPER REED, FOREVER FRIEND**

978-0-8050-9008-6